HAVING A BALL
with
IT'S A MADHOUSE

by the same author

ARE YOU LONESOME TONIGHT?
NO SURRENDER: A DEADPAN FARCE

HAVING A BALL

with

IT'S A MADHOUSE

ALAN BLEASDALE

First published in 1986 by
Faber and Faber Limited
3 Queen Square London WC1N 3AU

Phototypeset by Wilmaset Birkenhead Wirral
Printed in Great Britain by
Redwood Burn Limited, Trowbridge, Wiltshire

British Library Cataloguing in Publication Data

Bleasdale, Alan
Having a ball; It's a madhouse.
I. Title II. Bleasdale, Alan. It's a madhouse
822'.914[F] PR6052.L397

ISBN 0-571-14521-3

Library of Congress Cataloging-in-Publication Data

Bleasdale, Alan
Having a ball and it's a madhouse.
I. Title.
PR6052.L397H38 1986 822'.914 86-11502

ISBN 0-571-14521-3 (pbk.)

For Caroline Smith, Kenneth Alan Taylor and Michael Attenborough: three directors a writer can trust.

HAVING A BALL

'. . . Madam Prime Minister, I will make one further prediction – that the British people are once again about to pay homage to their beloved Sir Winston Churchill, by doing him the honour of proving him wrong, in showing the world that their finest hour is yet to come. And how he would have loved the irony of that, how proud it would have made him. So, ladies and gentlemen, I ask you to join in a toast to the memory of that great leader of free people, to his vision of bright sunlit uplands, a toast to his Britannia and all that she has been, and all that she will be, and to her finest hour, yet to come . . .'

Ronald Reagan

27 February 1981

British Embassy,
Washington

CHARACTERS

NURSE (John Gilbert)
SURGEON
LENNY ANDERSON
RITCHIE BURROWS
THREE FEMALE PATIENTS
ANAESTHETIST (Mr Martin)
MALCOLM THOMAS
DOREEN THOMAS
GEORGE HILL
JEAN HILL

Total of nine actors, six men, three women. (Jean Hill doubles as the women patients in the first act.)

The action takes place in a private clinic specializing in social and cosmetic surgery in the north-west of England.

There are three rooms seen on the stage, with a corridor running behind the rooms, linking them all. The action that takes place in the corridor can be seen through the plate-glass window/walls at the back of the Waiting Room. There are climbing plant frames in the corridor situated against the back wall/windows.

THE MEN'S WAITING ROOM: CENTRE STAGE
Imitation Habitat. Hessian on the walls. Six good-quality easy chairs, wood floors well polished, a coffee table laden with colour supplements and Country Life. *A pay phone and tannoy speaker close to each other. A* 'No Smoking' *sign prominent, perhaps on the back wall above the entrance. Lots of plants.*

THE PREPARATION ROOM. STAGE LEFT
A bed against side stage left wall, surrounded by Laura Ashley curtains and covers. A row of coat hooks, a left-behind umbrella, two hardbacked chairs, a small table, an internal phone, and a water jug and a glass. A small blind above the window in the door.

THE OPERATING THEATRE. STAGE RIGHT
Equipped in a modern manner but carrying only the bare essentials. The focus of the room is the operating table. There is an internal phone, a wash basin, a supply of paper towels, a waste bin, an instruments trolley, and swing doors.

The time is the present, Thursday afternoon.

Having a Ball was first presented at the Coliseum Theatre, Oldham, in March and April 1981. The cast was as follows:

NURSE	Jeffrey Longmore
SURGEON	Judith Barker
LENNY	David Ross
RITCHIE	Andrew Hay
PATIENTS	Lesley Nicol
ANAESTHETIST	Ian Mercer
MALCOLM	Cliff Howells
DOREEN	Lesley E. Bennett
GEORGE	Ted Morris
JEAN	Lesley Nicol
Director	Kenneth Alan Taylor
Designer	Jenny Blincow

ACT ONE

Darkness.

TANNOY: If a Mr Thomas is in the building would he please come to reception. Thank you.

(*Lights up.*

The Preparation Room and the Waiting Room are empty. In the Operating Theatre we see the SURGEON, *the male* NURSE, *a female* PATIENT, *and the* ANAESTHETIST. *The* SURGEON *is dressed in white trousers and a white loose-fitting smock that does not denote sex. The* NURSE *and the* ANAESTHETIST *are similarly dressed, except in light green. All three are wearing surgical hats. The* SURGEON *and the* ANAESTHETIST *still have face masks on.*

The WOMAN *on the operating table is unconscious, covered up apart from her head and shoulders. The white cloth covering her has absorbed a liberal degree of blood. The* SURGEON *is moving away from the operating table, holding her hands slightly away from herself. They too bear clear traces of blood. She walks towards the small wash basin at the side of the stage. The* NURSE *is already there, finishing washing his hands. The* SURGEON *waits for him to finish. And we see* LENNY ANDERSON *walk down the corridor from Reception, past the Preparation Room and enter the Waiting Room.*

He is tense and tentative. Walks towards the phone. Walks away. Approaches the phone again. Then hears the voice on the Tannoy. Walks straight out as the voice is heard. Goes off the way he came.)

Mrs Brady, your husband is at reception. Mr Thomas, we have someone waiting for you at reception. Mr Thomas, please.

THE OPERATING THEATRE

The NURSE *is drying his hands.* SURGEON *about to start washing hers.*

NURSE: Bit of a bleeder, wasn't she?

(*The* SURGEON *looks back at the* PATIENT. *As she does so, she flicks off her face mask and hat. We see for the first time that the* SURGEON *is a woman. Attractive, middle class, mid to late thirties.*)

SURGEON: Yes, I suppose she was. You never can tell. Not till you make them bleed . . .

(*The* SURGEON *turns away, begins to wash her hands as the* NURSE *dries his.*)

THE WAITING ROOM

We see RITCHIE BURROWS *arriving from Reception. He enters the room with a flourish and a smile, just in case someone is hiding behind a chair. He is a man in his mid-thirties, good strong features, expensive suit, tie and briefcase. He moves further into the room, stands facing out, rocking on his heels with his legs slightly open. He drops the briefcase on the floor, puts his hands in his trouser pockets and gently begins to disentangle his shaven testicles from his underpants.*

THE OPERATING THEATRE

The NURSE *completes the drying of his hands. He looks across at the* ANAESTHETIST.

NURSE: Go and put the next one under. We're all right here.

(ANAESTHETIST *hesitates a second and then exits.* NURSE *waits for him to go.*)

Where did you get him? The Youth Opportunity Programme?

SURGEON: He's twenty-six. And impressively well qualified.

NURSE: And impressively cheap . . .

(*The* NURSE *exits.*)

THE WAITING ROOM

We see RITCHIE BURROWS *open his jacket and waft the lapels about, sniffing casually as he does so. He opens his shirt beneath his tie and with his right hand inspects his left armpit. Smells his fingers. Frowns. Wide-legged, he picks his briefcase up, opens it and takes out a bottle of Brut. Is just about to splash it under his arms when the Tannoy goes again.*

TANNOY: Mr Thomas, Reception, *please.*

RITCHIE *looks around quickly and then continues to abuse the Brut, under his arms and then a quick squirt down inside his trousers. A brief pause. He then winces in extreme pain. He puts it away in his case and then sits down on one of the chairs. Gingerly. Takes out his newspaper, the* Daily Mail, *and begins reading.*

THE OPERATING THEATRE

As soon as RITCHIE *has dropped the Brut in his case we see the* NURSE *return with a trolley. He pushes it towards the operating table and places it at the side of the table. He picks up and glances at a list on a metal board hanging from the trolley as the* SURGEON *faces him.*

NURSE: Never mind, it's all downhill now.

SURGEON: (*Flatly*) Such as?

NURSE: Oh, a very interesting tattoo, a nose job, and as many vasectomies as you can manage.

(*As he speaks he unceremoniously throws the* PATIENT *on to the trolley.*)

SURGEON: Ah yes, the vasectomies. How I love vasectomies. That look of panic in their eyes when they find out . . . I'm a *woman.* What bliss.

NURSE: (*Moving away*) It could be worse, you could be doing something really boring like trying to save lives.

SURGEON: Hah hah hah.

(*The internal phone rings. The* NURSE, *moving the trolley out, is near to it. He answers, all sweetness.*)

NURSE: Good afternoon, new tits and noses limited . . .

SURGEON: Hoh hoh hoh.

NURSE: . . . Right. (*Puts phone down.*) 'Could one of the nursing staff kindly come down to reception please.' Christ, what a con job this place is. Which one of the nursing staff would you like to go – me or . . . me?

(*The* NURSE *exits with trolley and* PATIENT. *The* SURGEON *watches him go, and then exits herself, pushing furiously at the swing doors.)*

THE WAITING ROOM

As the NURSE *exits from the Operating Theatre, we see* RITCHIE BURROWS *put down his paper, lean forward and open his briefcase. As he does so, we see the* NURSE *cross from right to left in the corridor, going towards Reception.* RITCHIE *gets out a flask, undoes the cup top, unscrews the cap and starts pouring steaming coffee from the flask into the cup. We hear the Tannoy again.*

TANNOY: Mrs Thomas, can you kindly return to reception, please.

(RITCHIE *jumps and spills his coffee. He juggles with the cup, trying to avoid his suit, while desperately attempting to pour what is left of the coffee back into the flask, burning both hands and forming a puddle on the floor. He stands, hesitates, wipes his hands on the underneath of one of the seats, picks up his briefcase and flask, avoids the puddle and moves to a chair at the opposite side of the coffee table. Pretends that nothing has happened. Then looks sidelong at the puddle.* RITCHIE *stands up, takes his flask and briefcase and heads for the door.*

As he does this, we see MALCOLM THOMAS *in the corridor, entering from stage right. He is a man in his very early forties, in clothes of some expense but no fashion. He is carrying a large suitcase.* RITCHIE *reaches the door at the same time as* MALCOLM *is about to enter.)*

RITCHIE: *Hi!*

(MALCOLM *nods and walks straight past him.* RITCHIE *goes to walk down the corridor, stage left. Stops. Half hides behind the climbing plants in the corridor, waiting for* MALCOLM*'s reaction to the coffee.*

We see MALCOLM *see the coffee pool, look sharply towards the corridor. He catches* RITCHIE *looking in at him.* RITCHIE *turns and hastens off, stage left.* MALCOLM *puts the suitcase down, briefly surveys the room. He sees the* NURSE *walking past, returning from Reception.)*

MALCOLM: Nurse, one moment.
(*The* NURSE *enters casually.*)
Couple of matters, nurse. Firstly, I would like my suitcase put in a safe place under lock and key, and I would like the key. Now I know I'm . . .
(*As he talks, the* NURSE *walks past him and goes to the puddle. Looks at the puddle. Looks at* MALCOLM. *Looks back at the puddle.*)
I didn't do that.

NURSE: Oh, I'm sure you didn't.

MALCOLM: Right. Now I know I'm somewhat early for my appointment, but I was in the vicinity and thought it wiser that I was dropped here while the opportunity presented itself. And I just wondered if it was at all possible that my . . . operation could be moved forward slightly. (*Looks at the* NURSE.) That is possible, isn't it?

NURSE: No.

MALCOLM: Perhaps I should introduce myself. My name's . . .

NURSE: I know who you are, Mr Thomas.

MALCOLM: I'm sorry . . .?

NURSE: You closed the last hospital I worked in.

MALCOLM: *I* closed it?

NURSE: In your guise as honorary chairman of the local health authority.

MALCOLM: Now, these issues are naturally emotive, but . . .

TANNOY: Would Mrs Thomas *please* return to reception.
(MALCOLM *turns quickly towards the Tannoy, then back to the* NURSE.)

NURSE: Yes, your wife is here. She's looking for you, Mr Thomas. (*He picks up the suitcase.*) And we are looking for your wife. (*He moves towards the door.*) But don't worry, she shouldn't be too far away. Apparently she keeps falling over . . .

MALCOLM: Falling over?

NURSE: Yes. (*He reaches door, smiles at* MALCOLM.) I'll take you down to reception, shall I?

THE OPERATING THEATRE

We see the ANAESTHETIST *bringing in the next* PATIENT *on a trolley. She should have a 'Dolly Parton' wig on. He wheels her in so that her head faces out towards the audience and her feet point towards the swing doors.*

The SURGEON *enters quickly after them. Glances at the* PATIENT.

SURGEON: The tattoo?

ANAESTHETIST: The tattoo.

SURGEON: Where's the bearded lady and the three-legged man? But more to the point, where's Nurse Gilbert? (*She turns away and begins to prepare herself for the operation.*)

THE WAITING ROOM

We see LENNY ANDERSON *arrive back in the Waiting Room. Goes to the phone. Hesitates with his hand on the receiver. And the Tannoy blares out. He jumps back.*

TANNOY: Would Mrs Thomas please return to reception where her husband is now waiting for her. Thank you. (LENNY *glares at the Tannoy loudspeaker. Moves away. Notices the smell of Brut and coffee. Sniffs up, and walks straight into the puddle. Steps quickly away. Then approaches and skirts the puddle.* LENNY *bends down and sniffs the puddle. Dips his finger in, sniffs his finger. Wipes his finger on a chair. Stands up and walks away. Sits down suddenly on a chair.*)

LENNY: Now come on, this time!
(LENNY *mumbles towards the phone.*)
. . . OK, Monica . . . now listen, Monica, this is the one, this time . . . (*Looks at the Tannoy.*) . . . and don't you say a word . . .
(*He is dialling as he finishes talking. The pips go. He puts his money in. It jams.* LENNY *bangs the phone furiously. Perhaps releases the money, but too late. He slams the receiver down. Then searches his pockets. Takes out a jockstrap. Puts it back again with a shudder. He heads*

straight for the door. As he does so, we see RITCHIE *coming down the corridor, holding several paper towels. They meet at the doorway.*)

RITCHIE: Hi!

(LENNY *barely glances at him as he storms past.*)

Suit yourself . . .

(RITCHIE *goes over to wipe the puddle up.* LENNY *suddenly stops as he is about to go off, stage left. We see him staring through the Waiting Room window and the plants.* LENNY *slowly edges back into the room, after staring through the windows for a second or two. He nears* RITCHIE, *who finishes and turns to find* LENNY *looking at him, still and staring.*)

Ahhh, I . . . (*Indicates the puddle.*) . . . my coffee . . . it . . . on the . . .

(RITCHIE *mimes briefly.* LENNY *nods briefly. He moves around and then follows* RITCHIE *as he moves towards the door with his dripping paper towels.* RITCHIE *needs to say something/anything.*)

You er . . . don't happen . . . the er, gents toilet?

(LENNY *points stage left.* RITCHIE *raises a hand in acknowledgement, moves off. Glances behind himself once as he goes. Sees* LENNY *at the door still staring after him.* LENNY *moves into the room, shaking his head in disbelief.*)

LENNY: Well well well . . . after all these years.

(*Mumbling, he approaches the phone. Picks up the receiver, hesitates, sighs, puts receiver back, rests his head against the phone.*)

THE OPERATING THEATRE

The SURGEON, *her preparations complete, starts casually to investigate and search her* PATIENT *for the tattoo. She will, as* LENNY *continues in the Waiting Room, inspect the* PATIENT'S *hands, fingers, face, neck and shoulders. The* SURGEON *is moving down the trolley to look at the* PATIENT'S *feet. And is defeated. Glances at the* ANAESTHETIST.

SURGEON: Can you see a tattoo?

(*They both start looking. As they do, the* NURSE *returns from Reception, still carrying Malcolm Thomas's suitcase. The* SURGEON *and the* ANAESTHETIST *continue looking. They inspect the* PATIENT'*s ankles, calves, knees, then her upper legs.*)

SURGEON: Are you sure you've brought the right patient in?

ANAESTHETIST: Yes. (*But he's not at all sure.*)

(*The* SURGEON *lifts the body cover up. The* ANAESTHETIST *holds up one end as well. They both begin to peer under the cover as it falls over them. And the* NURSE *arrives back without the suitcase but with the patient's notes. The* NURSE *observes the two bobbing heads beneath the body cloth.*)

NURSE: I could have you both struck off for this, you know . . .

SURGEON: We can't find her tattoo.

(*The* NURSE *grins and approaches the trolley. Gives a nod to the* ANAESTHETIST *to take the other end of the* PATIENT.)

NURSE: A one a two a three!

(*He flings the* PATIENT *on to the operating table, but the* ANAESTHETIST *is behind him. The* PATIENT *ends up half on the table and half on the trolley. The* NURSE *shakes his head as the* ANAESTHETIST *finally gets the* PATIENT *on to the table. The* NURSE *then flicks the body cover back, takes hold of the* PATIENT'*s ankles and pushes her knees up. Then he opens her legs. Points between her legs.*)

There.

SURGEON: Where?

NURSE: There. That's what it says on the notes. (*Indicates the patient's notes.*) Amateur job, done with a needle and a laundry marker.

(*The* SURGEON *reads the notes briefly. Looks down at the body, looks up at the* NURSE. *Somewhat stunned. The* ANAESTHETIST *is peeping between both of them. The* NURSE *moves across so that he cannot see.*)

You're too young to see this. Other end.

(*The* ANAESTHETIST *moves towards the head of the* PATIENT.)

SURGEON: Ahhhh, I don't believe it. '*Sam Was Here*'!

NURSE: (*Pointing*) Plus a pierced heart.

SURGEON: But 'Sam Was Here' . . . Good God.

NURSE: Maybe he thought she was a tree trunk.

(*They both laugh. The* NURSE *looks again and shakes his head. Moves away towards the instrument trolley and moves it into position.*)

SURGEON: . . . No wonder she asked for a general . . . Right, I think we'll remove the heart first.

(*The* NURSE *and the* SURGEON *move into position above the* PATIENT. *And then they freeze.*)

THE WAITING ROOM

LENNY *stares at the phone and then at the Tannoy. He begins to dial again, talking to himself still.*

LENNY: . . . Right, this is it, Monica, I'll stay now, oh yes, I've got a reason to stay now . . . no really, my mind's made up . . . Monica. All right, Mon, it's me look love, do I . . . is that Philip or Linda screaming? . . . Ah, it's Jamie . . . Playschool was on strike again . . . of course . . . yes . . .

TANNOY: Would Mrs Thomas kindly return to Reception, please.

LENNY: Shut up! . . . No, not you, Monica, it was . . . (*He waves his hand helplessly.*) . . . a voice, Mon . . . Listen, this is important. I want to tell you the real reason why I've agreed to have a vasectomy . . . yes, I will get it done today, yes, I know I've come back complete every night this week, but today, I just feel today I might . . . pardon . . . *Mon*, don't use that word in front of the children . . . so, yes erm why am I phoning . . . well actually I'm phoning because (*Laughs nervously.*) . . . erm well what I really want to know, Mon is – is this my final decision? . . . No, I'm not being funny, I'm going mad, Monica, I am, I'm going mad *because I can't do anything! . . . I know*

I fixed the washing machine, I don't mean that!
(*He slams the phone down.*)
Goodbye, Monica.
(*He butts the phone twice.*)
(*Mimics*) 'You fixed the washing machine, Lenny.'
(*He howls long and loud, in exasperation and release. And the Tannoy blares.*)

TANNOY: Mrs Thomas, reception pl—
(*And* LENNY *puts his fist right through the speaker. As soon as he has started howling, we see* RITCHIE *enter the corridor. He stops behind the climbing plants and watches. As* LENNY *smashes the speaker he is startled but edges nearer to the door.* RITCHIE *stands at the door looking between* LENNY *and the Tannoy as* LENNY *moves away towards the chairs.*)

LENNY: . . . Monica, *Monica*, I'm worried about Nicaragua. . . .
(RITCHIE *looks around for* MONICA *or perhaps Nicaragua.*)
. . . 'But Nicaragua's a long way away Lenny, and there's nothing you can do about it, for a start your passport's expired, so there's no point in worrying about it, is there? Do you want tea or Horlicks?' . . . Oh Monica, Monica, why is it I can talk to you so much better when you're not there? . . . Listen, I want . . . I want to kill somebody Monica. Possibly myself, but nearly anybody will do.

RITCHIE: I'd better leave the room then!
(LENNY *whirls around, but after this first reaction, he stops still, then stands and begins to walk towards* RITCHIE, *his manner considerably composed.*)
Shouldn't talk to yourself, you know. People'll think . . .
(*He points towards his head, makes an idiot's face and noise.* LENNY *stares at him from a closer range than* RITCHIE *would wish.*) . . . Easily done though . . . I er . . . you know, I've always wanted to do that . . .
(RITCHIE *indicates the Tannoy but moves quickly away from* LENNY. *When* RITCHIE *turns around he finds,*

disconcertingly, that LENNY *is following him.* RITCHIE *turns to face him and gives* LENNY *his best 'Hail fellow well met' salesman's performance.*)

Well here we are – having a ball! (*Laughs.*) You know what they say – a snip in time saves nine! Hey what! (*Laughs, alone.*) Won't be long now, we'll all be singing 'Great Balls Of Fire' . . . Ah dear.

(LENNY *stares at him balefully.* RITCHIE *tries again.*)

Went past the nurse's canteen before – know what they were having for pudding? Plums! (*Laughs loudly and then illustrates the joke.*) Plums! . . . Oh yes . . . oh well. This is the Vasectomy Waiting Room, isn't it?

(LENNY *nods.* RITCHIE *picks up his briefcase and tries casually to move towards the Waiting Room doors.* LENNY *gets there before him, leans against the doors, folds his arms and stares at* RITCHIE. RITCHIE *turns back and goes to the furthest chair. Sits down and turns away from* LENNY. LENNY *moves into the centre of the room, picks up a chair, turns it around, sits down, with his arms folded on the head of the chair, stares at* RITCHIE.)

OPERATING THEATRE

As LENNY *completes his movement of the chair, we see the* SURGEON *move away from the operating table, and the* NURSE *go through the doors, quickly bringing a trolley back in. With the assistance of the* ANAESTHETIST *the* NURSE *throws the* PATIENT *on to the trolley. This time the* ANAESTHETIST *gets it right.*

NURSE: One, two, three . . . Very good . . .

(*Both* MEN *wheel the* PATIENT *out. As they do so, the intercom phone rings. The* SURGEON *picks it up.*)

SURGEON: Yes, yes, go on . . . how many weeks is she? . . . that's a lot of weeks, why has she waited *this* long? . . . Of course, the good old National Health, if in doubt, close a ward, preferably a women's ward . . . normally I would, as you know, but I have a problem . . . yes, the problem's my nurse . . . (*She laughs sardonically.*) . . . all right, if her situation is how you describe, and there are no alternatives, get her in this afternoon . . .

(*The* NURSE *comes back in with another* PATIENT *on the trolley, followed by the* ANAESTHETIST. *They get the* PATIENT *on to the table.*)

SURGEON: . . . I'll find a way, OK . . . Thank you.

NURSE: One, two, three.

SURGEON: (*Approaches the* NURSE.) John, change your mind.

NURSE: No.

SURGEON: As it happens, I need you.

NURSE: So do I. I need me. I need me more than you need me, nobody needs me more than me.

SURGEON: How terribly profound . . . (*The* NURSE *goes to move away. The* SURGEON *takes hold of his arm.*) Look, you know you're wrong.

NURSE: Do I? How do you know? . . . Anyway, two a penny, nurses.

SURGEON: Not good ones.

NURSE: (*Laughs.*) Well, you've tried everything else, I suppose flattery's worth a go. (*He moves back to the table.*) Let's get on with it, shall we?

(*The* SURGEON *indicates the* PATIENT *questioningly.*)

SURGEON: What is it?

NURSE: Nose job.

SURGEON: Right, pass me the hammer.

(*As the* NURSE *passes the implement – not a hammer – and they get into position, they freeze.*)

THE WAITING ROOM/CORRIDOR

We see LENNY *and* RITCHIE *as they were. We then see* DOREEN THOMAS *come from stage left and appear by the side window of the Waiting Room. She pulls at two of the canes for the climbing plants and peers into the Waiting Room. Then she slowly makes her way to the Waiting Room door. She is about to make her entrance when she slowly topples over backwards in the corridor. We see* MALCOLM THOMAS *enter frantically from the same direction. He picks* DOREEN *up and hustles her towards the Preparation Room.*

THE PREPARATION ROOM

We see MALCOLM *peer through the window into the room then open the door and thrust* DOREEN *through. We see that* DOREEN *is about fifteen years younger than her husband. She is beautiful and classy and drunk. But* not *staggering and slurring. Her accent is rooted in the North but it is not thick. She is wearing an outfit that is fashionable but not flash.*

They move into the room. She is smiling happily. MALCOLM *moves a chair into position.*

MALCOLM: Sit there. (*No reaction. He snaps his fingers.*) *There.*

DOREEN: Ever thought about being a dog handler, darling? (*She whistles, then growls at the chair, but finally sits down. He perhaps paces up and down.*)

MALCOLM: What are you doing here, Doreen?

DOREEN: I've come to see you, Malcolm.

MALCOLM: . . . What was all that in aid of?

DOREEN: A good cause.

MALCOLM: . . . Why did you fall over?

DOREEN: Which fall over are you referring to, angel?

MALCOLM: There, just there, in the corridor. You fell over.

DOREEN: Oh *that* one! That's right, you didn't see me fall over in Reception, did you?
(*Pause. He paces.*)

MALCOLM: What have you done with yourself today, Doreen?

DOREEN: Oh, nothing much. Took the kids to school, had breakfast, raped the milkman, washed the dishes . . .

MALCOLM: All right . . .

DOREEN: Oh, and then that nice man from the Gas Board wanted to see my flue again . . .

MALCOLM: All right, *all right.* Where are the children?

DOREEN: . . . I left them at your mother's. Leastways, I think it was your mother's. The house looked familiar . . .

MALCOLM: What are they doing at my mother's?

DOREEN: They're probably tied to a chair and locked in a bedroom if I know your mother. (*He starts to speak.*)

Malcolm, they're there because I want to talk to you. Leastways, I did want to talk to you. Till I saw you.

MALCOLM: Jesus . . . (*Quietly*) Give it to me. Now.

DOREEN: I beg your pardon!

MALCOLM: The bottle. I want the bottle.

DOREEN: What bottle? I didn't know *I* had to bring a sample.

(*He takes hold of her bulging and brightly coloured handbag. They tussle briefly as she makes a half-hearted attempt to stop him. He searches the bag and then brings out a large seven-eighths-full vodka bottle, wrapped in a women's magazine. Shows it to her.*)

Well, I never! How did that get there, light of my life?

MALCOLM: You're drunk. You're drunk *again*. At three thirty in the afternoon.

DOREEN: I am perfectly sober. Or, if you will, soberly perfect. (*She burps, holds her chest.*)

MALCOLM: Get up, go on, get up. Stand up.

(*He lifts her forcibly. She falls warmly all over him.*)

DOREEN: Oooooh. You're so rough with me. Just like the window cleaner.

MALCOLM: (*Pushing him*) Walk about, come on, walk up and down.

DOREEN: I have excused boots.

MALCOLM: Walk it off yourself. Now.

(*She starts walking up and down. Seemingly sober. She starts humming and half singing 'Only Sixteen'. The lyrics do not appeal to* MALCOLM. *He sits on the bed watching her.* DOREEN *approaches the doorway and the coathooks where the umbrella is hanging. She stops and leans her head against the back wall, takes hold of the umbrella and holds herself up. Stays still.*)

THE WAITING ROOM

RITCHIE, *his back turned as far as possible away from* LENNY, *shuffles in his pocket and gets his cigarettes and matches out. He strikes a match and lights his cigarette. As he does so,* LENNY *stands up and begins to look at the 'No Smoking' sign, as if it was a painting in an art gallery. He looks from two or three angles and then finally moves down towards* RITCHIE, *where he performs the actions at his side.* RITCHIE *finally looks at the sign, looks at his cigarette, looks at* LENNY, *nips the cigarette out on the floor, puts it back in the packet, turns away.* LENNY *carefully stands on the ashes of the cigarette on the floor, takes out a lighter and a packet of cigarettes, and lights one.* RITCHIE *stares at him bewildered as* LENNY *stands over him, puffing at the cigarette.*

LENNY: . . . You're Ritchie Burrows, aren't you?

RITCHIE: How . . . How did you know?

LENNY: I saw your picture in the *Manchester Evening News*. North-west's Salesman of the Year . . . for Farley's Rusks.

RITCHIE: (*Laughs involuntarily*) But that was . . . that was . . . 1983. Why would you remember that?

LENNY: Farley's Rusks played a very important part in my life at that time. It was like a religion – 'Our Farley's Rusks who are in handy-sized boxes, hallowed be thy name . . . Hail Farley's, blessed art thou amongst children's cereals . . .'

RITCHIE: You're pulling my leg.

LENNY: (*Flat and cold*) I went to school with you. (RITCHIE *looks up more carefully.* LENNY *half smiles.* RITCHIE *stands up to face him.*)

RITCHIE: Now wait a minute . . .

LENNY: You wouldn't remember me.

RITCHIE: No hang on, I'm good at faces . . . Graham Baxter! (RITCHIE *holds out his hand joyfully.* LENNY *takes it.*)

LENNY: He's dead.

RITCHIE: (*Removing his hand*) Are you sure?

LENNY: 'Course I'm sure.

RITCHIE: Shit. You know, I'm sorry . . . I mean, Manchester Grammar, big school . . . (*He retreats.*) . . . were we like . . . close?

LENNY: Alphabetically.

RITCHIE: It's well . . . it's nearly twenty years since . . .

LENNY: You wouldn't have remembered me if it had been twenty minutes ago. Big Jobs.

(RITCHIE *looks around. In disbelief and at* LENNY.)

RITCHIE: Hey, now, hold on. Enough of that, Jeez, I haven't been called . . . 'that name' since . . . You must have been one of those little bastards who hid behind corners and shouted . . .

LENNY: BIG JOBS!!!

(RITCHIE *doesn't know whether to run and hide or kill and run.*)

It was the only chance we had to get our own back. Big Jobs.

RITCHIE: It's not funny.

LENNY: I'm not laughing.

(RITCHIE *walks away. Progresses around the coffee table.*)

RITCHIE: It used to drive me mad. Everywhere I went in my last year, it was . . . it was . . .

LENNY: Big Jobs.

RITCHIE: Yeah, Big Jobs here and Big Jobs there . . . bloody Big Jobs everywhere. I went home one night and 'Big Jobs' was painted on our garden gate.

(RITCHIE *goes to sit down.*)

LENNY: I did that.

(RITCHIE *jumps up.*)

RITCHIE: You? (LENNY *nods affably.*) But *why*?

LENNY: It wasn't just me – it was all the other faceless little sods like me that you got your gang to torture.

RITCHIE: *Me*?

LENNY: Yes you. I had to eat custard and salt for you, I was pushed naked into the girls' changing room for you, I drank pond water for you, full of shite and frog spawn, walking home coughing tadpoles into my hankie. All for you . . . But we really had some plans of our own for you, Big Jobs. Ex-Lax in your chocolate pudding, ferrets in your jock strap, nitric acid in your aftershave . . . and then two of the science lads spent six months formulating and creating a bomb to put in your briefcase.

(LENNY *has sat on the edge of the coffee table, facing* RITCHIE.)

RITCHIE: *What*?

LENNY: Yeah, one of them blew himself up on the number nine bus one morning . . . Coming to school.

RITCHIE: Ernie Reddock! I remember that! Who was the other one?

LENNY: I don't remember. Poor old Ernie. He was in hospital for weeks. Never came back to school till the autumn term, did his O levels in the ward, and the bus company sued his parents. Something about non-declaration of a parcel . . .

RITCHIE: Was . . . was that supposed to be for. . . ?

LENNY: Oh aye.

RITCHIE: Bugger me sideways . . . A . . . bomb?

LENNY: A bomb.

RITCHIE: A real . . . bomb.

LENNY: (*Nods.*) I saw the hole in the bus. It was big.

RITCHIE: They wanted to . . . kill me?

LENNY: I believe that was the intention. At the time.

RITCHIE: But why?

LENNY: (*Almost warmly*) Because you made our lives a living hell. You were a monster. (*Turns away.*) Funny really. I always thought you'd join the police force . . .

(LENNY *sits on a chair facing* RITCHIE *across the coffee table. Appears utterly relaxed.*)

RITCHIE: But I wasn't like that. I wasn't like that at all.

LENNY: Course you weren't. It's just that the rest of us thought you were.

(*Pause.*)

RITCHIE: What was your name again?

LENNY: Lenny Anderson.

RITCHIE: (*Slowly*) . . . Lenny Anderson . . . (*Shakes his head.*) . . . What did they call you, you know, at school?

LENNY: Nothing. I was just an also-ran, remember?

someone to hit in passing – like horse racing on the television – the horse that comes in seventh – getting the buggery beaten out of it all the way – still seventh. Never mentioned once by Peter O'Sullivan.

RITCHIE: You . . . you couldn't have been like you say you were. Not the way you are now. I mean, yeah all right, so you talk to yourself, don't we all . . . but I couldn't have scared you. Not me.

LENNY: (*Throws it away*) Most of us are cowards most of the time. Until we have no choice. And all the choices seem to be going.

(RITCHIE *nods sagely but hasn't a clue what* LENNY *is talking about.* LENNY *stubs his cigarette out on the floor and backheels it under his chair. Folds his arms and stares at* RITCHIE *who looks away from him.*)

THE PREPARATION ROOM

DOREEN *faces the wall, leaning on the umbrella.*

DOREEN: . . . Let me go home.

MALCOLM: I would if I thought you would go home.

DOREEN: I will. Promise. (*She turns and walks towards him.*)

MALCOLM: You're staying where I can see you.

DOREEN: Going to take me in the operating theatre with you, are you, Malcolm? That will be nice. Hold your stiff little . . . hand.

MALCOLM: There is a difference between being clever and being smart, Doreen. Keep walking.

DOREEN: Ahhhh, married life, there's nothing quite like it. Whoever called it an institution certainly knew what she was talking about . . . (*Still walking up and down*) . . . Let me go home. Please.

MALCOLM: Keep walking.

(MALCOLM *clasps his hands together angrily.*)

DOREEN: (*Close to him, above him*) You know . . . the sad thing is, when I married you, you were someone to look up to. I looked up to you, Malcolm. Now, you'd have to stand on a mountain.

(MALCOLM *jumps up quickly.* DOREEN *flinches and moves a pace or so away.* MALCOLM *pushes her towards the chair, forces her to sit down at the table. He moves the jug and the glass towards her.*)

MALCOLM: Drink this.

DOREEN: (*Sniffing it*) Water? I don't drink water. Not on its own, Malcolm. Furthermore, treasure, I am, as you know, totally opposed to fluoride in the . . .

(*He is ignoring her, and as she talks he picks up her purse out of her handbag. Starts to empty out her money. She stops and watches him.*)

The Territorial Army teaches you so much . . .

MALCOLM: Drink that and you can go home. Now that the pubs and the banks are shut.

(*He puts her money and bank card in his coat pocket, except for some loose change, which he drops on the table.*)

There's thirty pence, you can get the bus home.

DOREEN: Three days and nights you've been away, Malcolm.

MALCOLM: I haven't been on holiday, Doreen. I've been working, it was a survival exercise. As you well know.

DOREEN: Oh, you've been 'exercising'; how do you keep fit at the end of the world, darling? Digging graves? In your brand new special issue suit?

MALCOLM: Don't talk about things you know nothing about, Doreen.

DOREEN: Three days and nights. Three days and nights I slept with the children, Malcolm. Well, they slept with me. Actually I didn't sleep at all. *You bastard. I needed you.*

MALCOLM: Doreen, I . . .

(*Pause.* MALCOLM *pours water into the glass.*)

DOREEN: . . . Anyway, I came here to do you a favour, Malcolm. Just think, now I'm here I can drive my little wounded soldier home afterwards.

MALCOLM: You're in no fit state.

DOREEN: Neither will you be in a couple of hours. Your legs'll be so far apart, the clutch'll have to be on the passenger's side.

MALCOLM: I'll cope with that.

DOREEN: Ah, it's a man's life . . .

(She looks at the water in the glass. Examines and tests the density but never quite drinks it. MALCOLM *sits back on the bed, watching her.)*

THE WAITING ROOM

RITCHIE *and* LENNY *sit as they were.* RITCHIE *is getting twitchy. He starts drumming his fingers on the wooden arm of the chair.* LENNY *looks at his fingers, looks up at* RITCHIE*'s face, then back at his fingers.* RITCHIE *stops. Immediately begins to crack his knuckles.* LENNY *leans forward and looks again.* RITCHIE *stops. Puts his hands in his lap, then takes them quickly out. Goes to bite his nails, stops as* LENNY *looks at him.* RITCHIE *stands up, puts his hands behind his back, walks up and down, whistling tunelessly.* LENNY *sits back and takes his* Guardian *newspaper out. Looks at the front page. Registers dismay.*

LENNY: Kinnell . . .

(LENNY *turns quickly to the sports pages.* RITCHIE *is now desperate to talk about anything.)*

RITCHIE: The *Guardian*, hey?

LENNY: Yeah. The *Guardian*. So?

RITCHIE: Oh, nothing, nothing . . . I bought the *Guardian*. Once . . . Married, er Lenny, kids?

(LENNY *looks up at him over the top of his newspaper.)*

Hah, course you are! Otherwise you wouldn't . . . be here . . .

LENNY: *(With pointed politeness)* How did *you* become Salesman of the Year?

RITCHIE: *(Just happy to talk)* Oh well, actually, I was giving the manageress of this chemist's in Swinton a good seeing-to, know what I mean? *(He winks at* LENNY, *makes a sexual gesture with his upturned fist.)* . . . a bit of the old charm, you know – After Eights, After Dinner and After her husband had gone to the pub. *(He laughs.*

LENNY *can hardly hide his contempt.*) . . . Yeah, before she knew it, she'd ordered 13,000 packets of rusks . . . It was going great till her boss opened the stock cupboard . . . I don't work for Farley's Rusks any more.

LENNY: No?

RITCHIE: I work in insurance now.

LENNY: Good for you.

RITCHIE: Although you know, I'm always looking around . . . it's a bit tight at the moment . . . What do *you* do? Lenny.

LENNY: I'm a scientist. In a biscuit factory.

RITCHIE: A what?

LENNY: Yes, it does seem like a contradiction in terms, doesn't it? Like military intelligence . . . What it really means is that I make sure we don't poison the nation with an excess of calcium phosphate, and I try to stop the loose screws, nits and cigarette ends turning up in the fruit macaroons.

(LENNY *puts his paper back up.* RITCHIE *starts pacing again.*)

RITCHIE: . . . I haven't given it much thought, you know – the operation, put it out of my mind . . . rang up a fortnight ago, booked myself in, told the boss I'd be away for a day or so, moved the wife into the spare room, warned the girlfriend not to expect too much for a couple of nights . . .

(RITCHIE *laughs, once more alone.*)

. . . didn't really sink in till I was lying in the bath shaving myself this morning . . . wife stood watching me, suggesting I used the electric razor . . . (*Laughs. Waits for a reaction.*) *In the bath. Electric.* (*Mimes electrocution.*) Eh what – be all right when it's over. Know what I mean? No worries. Heh heh. Free as the wind. Firing blanks all over Lancashire.

(LENNY *looks up from his paper. Nods.* RITCHIE *sits on the edge of the coffee table near* LENNY.)

RITCHIE: Oh yes. After all, it's nothing much, is it? A minor operation, that's all . . . 'bum-bum' – 'snip-snip' – lie down for half an hour and walk home bandy.

LENNY: (*Flat*) Well, if a recent president of the CBI can die under a general anaesthetic in a private hospital having his cartilage removed, anything is possible.

RITCHIE: . . . Great. Thanks . . .

(*He stands up and moves away.*)

LENNY: And then there's the septicaemia.

RITCHIE: The what? Septicaemia? With a vasectomy?

LENNY: Well, not many get that. Very few in fact.

RITCHIE: I should hope not.

LENNY: Yeah. Mostly, it's septic balls.

RITCHIE: Get lost!

(LENNY *stands up and approaches* RITCHIE. *'Sincerely'.*)

LENNY: Nobody's told you about that?

RITCHIE: Nobody's told me because it isn't true . . . Is it?

LENNY: Say no more, that's me. No point in worrying you now. (*Slaps* RITCHIE *on the shoulder, then glances at his watch.*) Not now . . .

(RITCHIE *retreats to a chair.* LENNY *grins at him, leans against the telephone.*)

THE OPERATING THEATRE

The 'nose job' is over. The NURSE *moves the instrument trolley away. The* SURGEON *moves towards him. The* ANAESTHETIST *is in attendance.*

NURSE: Bring on the men . . . (*Holds up a knife.*) 'This is what they want!'

SURGEON: John. There is one more woman. Short notice. Some time today.

NURSE: And?

SURGEON: Urgent.

NURSE: And? Come on.

(*The* NURSE *looks towards the* ANAESTHETIST.)

Don't just stand there, go and put someone else under.

ANAESTHETIST: (*Half goes, then turns back*) There is no one else.

NURSE: Go and practise on the tropical fish then. Go on.

ANAESTHETIST: But . . . (*Indicates the patient.*)

NURSE: (*Moving him towards the door*) This isn't medical school, son, it's an assembly line. Wait outside.

(*The* ANAESTHETIST *reluctantly goes.*)

And?

(*The anaesthetized* WOMAN *on the table starts mumbling and fidgeting slightly. The* NURSE *glances at her quickly.*)

SURGEON: Although I may well be wasting my time, I'm asking you to be the nurse in attendance.

NURSE: There being no one else here.

SURGEON: Yes.

NURSE: Meaning it's something I don't want to do any more, surgery I no longer wish to be connected with.

SURGEON: Oh grow up.

NURSE: What?

SURGEON: Would I be asking you if it was a hare lip or a clubbed foot? Hammered toes, a new nose . . . I wouldn't ask you. I wouldn't *need* to ask you.

PATIENT: (*Suddenly, in high upper-class tones*) I only like butter on my bread, Roger!

(*The* NURSE *and the* SURGEON *double-take towards the* PATIENT. *Then they both turn back to each other. They become, despite the interventions of the* PATIENT, *very heated.*)

NURSE: Find someone else to do it. You know that's why I've resigned.

SURGEON: I don't think I can. It's very late. Any further delay, according to my report and . . .

NURSE: Let it live then.

SURGEON: That's not my decision. It could be in a few days' time but not now. It's the woman's request, her decision. Her choice.

NURSE: The unborn child has no choice.

SURGEON: Ohhh! You shouldn't read propaganda – you're too easily influenced.

NURSE: You've had my notice in writing. This is my last day.

PATIENT: I mean for heaven's sake, Roger, who do you think you are?

NURSE: Do you hear me?

PATIENT: Well, get someone else to do it if that's what you want. I'd have to be double-jointed for a start.

NURSE: I've had enough of this bastard place. I'm going back to what I know, I'm going back to looking after life, not tarting it up or killing it.

SURGEON: Meanwhile, you're going to assist in the sterilization of half a dozen men this afternoon. I'd call that quite a killing.

NURSE: There is a difference between removing the *opportunity* to produce life and removing the life that is already produced. *You* know that.

SURGEON: Yes, one operation is £45 and the other is £97.50.

NURSE: Ah come on, there must be more to life than giving women new noses and tits that stare at the ceiling.

SURGEON: (*Cool*) There is – there're face lifts, eye bag removals, the flattening of ears and the re-shaping of chins and cheekbones. Not to mention tattoos in private places, warts, abortions and several sterilizations daily.

NURSE: Great. Absolutely great. Medic—

PATIENT: So? So? I might have a big nose, but you've got a little prick.

NURSE: I beg your pardon!

PATIENT: A very little prick!

NURSE: Shut up!

(*The* NURSE *hurls the* PATIENT *off the table on to the trolley. As the* PATIENT *continues, he hurtles the trolley out of the operating theatre.*)

PATIENT: I know my pricks, Roger, and yours is definitely small, minute even . . . I can get my nose done, Roger – what are you going to do about your prick? Hey? Hey? Hah hah hah hah . . .

(*The* NURSE *re-enters.*)

NURSE: Is that all?

SURGEON: Yes, but in the meantime, Mr Gilbert, will you complete the work you anticipated doing today, while I try to organize the possibility of a replacement for the . . . the other case . . . surgery.

NURSE: Yes.

SURGEON: Thank you.

(*The* NURSE *goes out. The* SURGEON *sweeps after him.*)

THE PREPARATION ROOM

DOREEN *has not made much progress with the water.*

MALCOLM: . . . We'd have no worries if you drank spirits this slow . . . come on, come on . . . (*He advances on her. She doesn't respond.*) . . . Doreen . . . *Doreen.*

DOREEN: Doreen. Bloody Doreen. All the names under the sun and my mother picked Doreen. I mean, how can you go to a Hunt Ball or a dinner at the Town Hall and be announced as . . . 'Doreen'.

MALCOLM: (*Inevitably*) Doreen . . .

(*He winces, but still moves towards her.*)

DOREEN: Call me Clarissa and I'll make it worth your while . . .

MALCOLM: Listen to me – *listen to me.*

DOREEN: (*Out of the blue*) You talk in your sleep, you know.

MALCOLM: What? Who does?

DOREEN: You do. Every night.

MALCOLM: (*Disbelieving*) Since when?

DOREEN: Since that sad day you became a man of position and power. You talk about your work. And its . . . ultimate potential. In your sleep. 'Attack. Warning Red.'

MALCOLM: What?!

DOREEN: You think I don't know, don't you?

MALCOLM: *Look*, I am here in this clinic because I am about to have a vasectomy, not because I have bad dreams or you have a drink problem . . .

DOREEN: It's no problem . . .

MALCOLM: We are not supposed to be in this room – we are only in this room because you fell over – this room will no doubt be used soon. . . .

DOREEN: All those naked men . . .

MALCOLM: *Are you listening to me?*

DOREEN: No.

MALCOLM: Doreen, I am supposed to be in the Waiting Room, waiting. And I want to go into the Waiting Room and wait. Do you understand? I want you sober, I want you home where no one can see you, and I want to get this over and done with . . .

DOREEN: Excuse me, dear . . .

MALCOLM: I'm doing this for you, you know – for you! Or more like, because of you. I do everything lately because of what you do to me.

DOREEN: Listen, Malcolm . . .

MALCOLM: I stay out late because of you – I go away because of you – I am ashamed because of you – I think twice about bringing people home because of you.

DOREEN: Darling, just one . . .

(MALCOLM *grabs hold of the vodka bottle, waves it in front of* DOREEN. *She can't take her eyes off it for some seconds, but still joins in his 'because of you' comments as he continues, saying 'because of me'.*)

MALCOLM: I look through the house for vodka bottles because of you – I'm having this vasectomy because of you, do you understand that? *Do you?*

DOREEN: (*As wild as he is*) Yes, of course I do. I do understand, Malcolm. It's very good of you. Cheers Big Ears! Saluté! (*She calms.*) Here's to you . . . and here's to me. Here's to the sixteen-year-old virgin and the seventeen-year-old mother . . . here's to the parties she never went to and the men she never met and the affairs she never had . . . here's to your first wife . . . never has there been a woman so glad to lose her man. Yes . . . (*Holds her glass up.*) . . . Oh, and by the way, Malcolm, I think you should know, I'm going to be sick.

MALCOLM: . . . Sick?

(*He looks around for something to take the consequences.*)

DOREEN: You know – 'wurrrrrrgggghhhhhh!' Very soon as a matter of fact. (*She puts her head down.*) I told you you made me sick . . .

MALCOLM: If you're . . .

(DOREEN *groans heavily.* MALCOLM *searches for a container. He looks under the bed and then brings the water jug down to her as she leans forward. She pushes it away from herself. Puts her head in her hands.* MALCOLM *grabs the magazine off the table, places it open on the floor in front of her. He turns and races for the door. As he does so, we see* DOREEN *turn over the page.* MALCOLM *turns back and nearly catches her reading. She starts coughing. He races out. At first he goes off stage left towards Reception.* DOREEN *hears the door close. She reaches out for the vodka bottle, holds it to her chest lovingly.*)

DOREEN: Ahhhh, baby . . .

THE WAITING ROOM

RITCHIE *finally cannot resist it.*

RITCHIE: Who . . . who told you about you know before – the er septic er . . .

LENNY: (*Moves happily towards him.*) Friend of mine. Said the worst bit though was ringing them up here, whispering . . .

(*As* LENNY *mimes a phone call,* MALCOLM *bursts into the room and hears* LENNY.)

LENNY: '. . . Excuse me, sorry to bother you, but I think I've got septic testicles. . . .'

(MALCOLM *backs out of the room, fast. Exits left towards and briefly past the Operating Theatre.* LENNY *and* RITCHIE *watch him briefly.*)

. . . anyway, they were very pleasant about it. Said it wasn't at all unusual, yeah, apparently over 40 per cent of their vasectomy patients go septic to some degree afterwards . . . made him feel a lot more at ease that did.

(RITCHIE *looks away from* LENNY. *Closes his legs.*)

THE OPERATING THEATRE

We see MALCOLM *enter. He sees the operating table. Backs out and goes out and off, stage right.*

THE CORRIDOR

We see an extremely old man and a much younger woman as they cross the corridor.

GEORGE: It can't be far away. Which floor did she say, Jean?

JEAN: Second, love.

GEORGE: What?

JEAN: *Second.*

THE PREPARATION ROOM

We focus on DOREEN *as we hear her giggle. She goes to drink out of the vodka bottle, then stops. She holds the bottle, looks at the water jug. She puts the bottle down and stands. Looks about. Runs to the umbrella, opens it out. It has a rip in it. She closes it and throws it away. Goes to the table again. Looks at the bottle and the jug. Looks around. Sees the magazine on the floor. She kneels down, grabs the magazine, rapidly folds it into a cone shape, glancing at the door, perhaps singing 'we can work it out', highly animated. Then she pours the water from the jug into the cone. Then she pours the vodka from the bottle into the jug. Then she releases the tip of the cone into the vodka bottle, so that the water pours into the vodka bottle. Job completed, highly delighted, she throws the magazine behind the table and at the side of the bed. She sits down, drinks from the water jug. A stiff one. Salutes* MALCOLM.

DOREEN: Cheers, Malcolm.

THE WAITING ROOM

LENNY *re-opens the conversation, still close to* RITCHIE.

LENNY: You know why, don't you? You know why you go septic around there? The clinic told him on the phone. It's a very dirty area, your erogenous zone. Very dirty indeed . . .

RITCHIE: Yeah yeah . . .

LENNY: . . . Attract germs like flies around a cow pat, erogenous zones do . . .

RITCHIE: Look . . .

LENNY: And then there's the internal bleeding, just a slow trickle no one can see . . .

RITCHIE: Leave it, will you.

LENNY: They do say a severed artery is no problem – the blood hits you in the face, but those little blood vessels . . .

RITCHIE: I SAID LEAVE IT!

LENNY: No chance, not now, Big Jobs. You're on your own these days . . .

(RITCHIE *stands and almost prods* LENNY. *Almost.*)

RITCHIE: Two things – don't call me Big Jobs, and secondly –

(*And* MALCOLM *rushes back in.*)

MALCOLM: A bin – a bin – where can I get a bin?

(LENNY *and* RITCHIE *look around, then look at* MALCOLM.)

LENNY: Where can he get a bin, Big Jobs?

(MALCOLM *can't wait. Out he runs again. Towards stage left.* LENNY *talks as he leaves the room.*)

And secondly. . . ?

RITCHIE: Ah forget it, you're not worth the breath.

THE PREPARATION ROOM

DOREEN *drinking. We see* MALCOLM *run past. We see him go. We see him return and peer in through the window in the door.* DOREEN *sees him. Groans.* MALCOLM *half goes but then races back into the room. He grabs the vodka bottle and races out again.*

DOREEN: Hurry up, Malcolm, I can't wait much longer . . .

(*He goes even faster. She laughs and salutes him again, then stands. She staggers slightly for the first time. Approaches the bed, drops the jug carefully on the floor. Stands on the bed and brings the curtains around herself, then suddenly collapses out of sight on to the bed.*)

THE WAITING ROOM

As DOREEN *disappears dramatically behind the curtain, the* NURSE *approaches the Waiting Room from stage right. He is carrying three dressing gowns and a clipper board.*

NURSE: Good afternoon, gentlemen. (*Sees* LENNY. *Smiles.*) You here again?

LENNY: This time. This is the one. I've had strict orders – don't come home unless you've been cut open.

NURSE: (*Amused*) We won't give you a form to fill in, Mr Anderson, we've already got three of yours in the office. Mr. . . ?

RITCHIE: Burrows.

NURSE: Good. Still a couple more to come, but . . . (*He ticks him off and then gives him a form. Moves towards the door as he talks.*) If you could answer these questions, Mr Burrows . . .

LENNY: You know, C of E, RC, Atheist or Ape, where's your favourite cemetery, what shall we do with your vital organs later today . . . sign here for your kidneys . . . (RITCHIE *takes a pen out and sourly starts filling the form in.*)

THE PREPARATION ROOM

The NURSE *enters. He looks curiously at the mess on the table, the handbag, some spilt water, the loose change. Then he turns away to put the dressing gowns on the hooks on the back wall. As he does so, we see* DOREEN*'s hand slide out from underneath the curtains around the bed and grab the water jug, taking it back behind the curtains. The* NURSE *turns and walks past the bed. He is just about to open the curtains when he sees the soggy magazine on the floor at the side of the bed. He moves to pick it up. As he does so,* MALCOLM *charges in through the doorway, holding an aluminium bedpan. He runs to the curtained side of the bed. As soon as he sees the* NURSE, MALCOLM *puts the bedpan behind his back.*

MALCOLM: He— Hello! I'm er sorry, I er thought you were my wife . . .

NURSE: I'm not your wife I'm afraid. I'm not even a woman.

MALCOLM: No. Er, quite. I er . . .

(*He really wants to pull the curtains across, but sees the* NURSE *looking at him somewhat curiously.* MALCOLM *turns, bends down and drops the bedpan underneath the spare chair. He picks up his wife's handbag and scrapes the thirty pence off the table into her bag, talking.*)

My wife's what-nots . . . she'll be around somewhere . . . no doubt . . . I'll er . . .

NURSE: You seem to have forgotten something, Mr Thomas.

MALCOLM: Pardon? Have . . . Have I?

(*The* NURSE *takes a yale key out. Shows it to* MALCOLM.)

NURSE: Your suitcase. I locked it away.

MALCOLM: Er, yes, I er . . . thank you.

NURSE: Something important inside, sir?

MALCOLM: I beg your pardon?

NURSE: I just thought there must be something important inside if you . . .

MALCOLM: I don't think that's any business of yours. Where have you put it?

NURSE: Second room on the left past the operating theatre. The room marked 'Laundry'.

(*The* NURSE *moves towards the door and waits for* MALCOLM. MALCOLM *puts the key in his pocket and stays where he is. He finally finds the urge irresistible and flings the curtains across the bed wide open. But no* DOREEN. MALCOLM *turns and smiles limply at the* NURSE. *Inspects the pillow for comfort and the mattress for spring. He then follows the* NURSE *out of the room.*)

THE WAITING ROOM

MALCOLM *enters. With handbag, and fraught. He walks across between* RITCHIE *and* LENNY, *carrying the handbag as he would a briefcase. They watch fascinated. He sits down and puts the handbag on his knee.* LENNY *looks at* RITCHIE, *whistles, swivels his eyes and goes to join* RITCHIE. MALCOLM *notices, notices the handbag on his knee and furiously shoves the handbag to the side of his chair. And the* NURSE *re-enters, from stage left.*

NURSE: Sorry, Mr Thomas, Reception would like to see you again. If you don't mind.

MALCOLM: . . . Now?

NURSE: Yes, please. Just a small matter.

LENNY: Of a cheque for £45. Dead men don't pay, you see.

RITCHIE: Christ . . .

(MALCOLM *is hardly amused either. He stares at* LENNY *until he has to go past him with his handbag. Then looks away. The* NURSE *takes him past the Preparation Room and off.*)

THE PREPARATION ROOM

As MALCOLM *disappears and the* NURSE *walks across, we see* DOREEN *slide out from under the bed.*

DOREEN: . . . 'My wife's what-nots.' (*She laughs.*) . . . and what's more, I can get home on my own . . . (*She addresses a chair as if* MALCOLM *was sitting on it, even though she is moving towards the door, jug in hand.*) . . . I don't need you, sod you and your special suit and your secret suitcase . . . I have influence too . . . I have an account at the off licence . . . they like me in the off licence, I'm their friend . . .

(*She reaches the door, mainly by bumping into it. Goes into the corridor towards the Waiting Room, carrying her jug.*)

THE WAITING ROOM

We see DOREEN *going past. Then looking in at the two men. She sees no* MALCOLM. *Opens the door, leans mock-provocatively against it.*

DOREEN: Mmmmmmmmmmmmmmm! See you later, boys . . .

(*She spoils her exit slightly by nearly tripping over the door as she pushes away from it, but she goes off stage right. And both men stand and move to the door, leaning out to see her go.*)

LENNY: So this is why private clinics are so expensive . . .

RITCHIE: It's all right, she was a man at ten o'clock this

morning.

(LENNY *laughs genuinely.* RITCHIE *joins in delighted.*)

LENNY: Very good. For you, Big Jobs.

RITCHIE: *Don't.* I'm telling you – don't!

(RITCHIE *grabs his cigarettes out of his pocket, lights one as* LENNY *circles him.*)

LENNY: You're not the same, are you – you're really not – fifteen, twenty years ago I'd have had a black eye and a dead rat down my back for that. Do you remember the time you got someone to put maggots in my . . .

RITCHIE: Why don't you shut it!

(RITCHIE *turns away.* LENNY *follows him.*)

LENNY: Well you see, I'm treating you as a sort of test-case . . .

RITCHIE: You being a sort of bleeding head case . . .

LENNY: No, I decided recently, and probably twenty years too late, not to let myself be pushed around. With quite pleasing results actually.

RITCHIE: The Shrimp's Revenge, hey? Pillock.

LENNY: You never know . . . 'Today Big Jobs Burrows, Tomorrow Ze World!'

(*They both stare at each other.* LENNY *flops happily into a chair.*)

THE OPERATING THEATRE

The SURGEON *enters briskly. Goes straight to the internal phone. Dials.*

SURGEON: I've just picked a young woman off the floor outside the operating theatre, she's in the ladies' prep room at the moment refusing to let go of a water jug. Would you kindly send someone down there, and if you see Mr Gilbert, tell him I want to see him. Thank . . . ah, wait, any news about a new nurse? . . . Right.

(*As the* SURGEON *nears the end of her conversation, we see the* NURSE *cross from left to right in the corridor. The* SURGEON *reaches the doors of the Operating Theatre as he has just gone past. She shouts after him.*)

SURGEON: John . . . John.

(*The* NURSE *enters.*)

NURSE: Yes.

SURGEON: There's a strange woman in a state of collapse in the ladies' prep room. I want her out of the way, preferably out of the building. I have to interview a patient.

NURSE: All right.

SURGEON: (*Looks at her watch.*) Listen, I'm obviously going to be delayed but I want the vasses ready to go when I get back.

NURSE: I'll start them off then. (*He turns away.*)

SURGEON: John, I haven't got another nurse yet.

(*No answer.*)

I don't think I'm going to get another nurse today.

NURSE: Tough.

(*He goes out without looking at her. The doors swing towards her. She pushes at them angrily and goes out.*)

THE WAITING ROOM

MALCOLM *re-enters, with handbag.* RITCHIE *is still smoking.* MALCOLM *looks at the sign.* MALCOLM *crosses by him towards a chair. Speaks with authority.*

MALCOLM: Do you mind not smoking.

LENNY: Ah, go and play with your handbag.

MALCOLM: I'm not talking to you.

LENNY: I'm not smoking.

MALCOLM: I am talking to him. Please do you mind not smoking.

(RITCHIE *hesitates.*)

LENNY: Kill him, Big Jobs. Push him in a pond. Attaboy!

RITCHIE: Look! . . .

(RITCHIE *moves across* MALCOLM *and grabs hold of* LENNY *by his shirt.* LENNY *cries out happily.*)

LENNY: 'DON'T HIT ME BIG JOBS, *PLEASE!*' Ah, just

like old times.

(RITCHIE *throws* LENNY *away from himself. Draws heavily on his cigarette and walks straight into* MALCOLM.)

MALCOLM: Can you please put that cigarette out. You might care to kill yourself if you want to, but I don't . . .

(RITCHIE *throws the cigarette on the floor and stamps on it. Sits down on a chair, facing out.*)

Thank you.

(MALCOLM *sits down as well.* LENNY *walks behind both of them. Takes out his packet of cigarettes. Lights one. Holds the smoke in his mouth as he approaches* MALCOLM *and* RITCHIE *sitting facing out. As he gets near to them he lets out a billow of smoke that settles between* RITCHIE *and* MALCOLM. MALCOLM *reacts first and turns angrily to* RITCHIE. *Who stares at him helplessly/hopelessly.* MALCOLM *then turns around and sees* LENNY.)

(*To* RITCHIE) Now look here. (*To* LENNY) Really, how childish.

(LENNY *draws heavily on his cigarette, lets the smoke fall about* MALCOLM, *then flicks the ash on the floor.*)

LENNY: Pity you didn't find that bin.

(*And* LENNY *promptly sits on* RITCHIE*'s knee like a small boy.* RITCHIE *pushes him away angrily.* MALCOLM *turns his back on both of them. And* DOREEN *stoops farcically past the Waiting Room heading for the Preparation Room. She is seen by both* RITCHIE *and* LENNY, *who walk towards the doors.* MALCOLM *then turns around questioningly.* RITCHIE *looks at him, shrugs his shoulders. Both* LENNY *and* RITCHIE *sit down.* RITCHIE *sits near* MALCOLM, LENNY *at right angles. Smokes heavily. We see* MALCOLM *stare angrily at him.*)

THE PREPARATION ROOM

DOREEN *opens the door to the room suddenly. As if wanting to catch a naked man. Disappointed and seeming to be 'over-tired' at last, she drops the jug on to the table and drops into bed, dragging the curtains around herself.*

RITCHIE: (*To* MALCOLM, *who is staring evilly at* LENNY *who is sending a stream of smoke towards* MALCOLM) Are you in for the, er . . . you know, the er old plums into prunes touch, hey? Every one guaranteed a blank. What! Hey! They'll be queuing at your door you know. Women. Did you know that? Drop the word in the office, let them know, that won't be the only thing that'll drop! Hey, hey!

MALCOLM: Have you ever considered that it might be a socially responsible act?

RITCHIE: Er, yeah. That as well.

(MALCOLM *stands and approaches* LENNY, *who cheerfully looks up at him.*)

LENNY: . . . You er will tell me when I'm supposed to be scared, won't you?

(LENNY *grins affably at* MALCOLM.)

MALCOLM: I have a sign in my office – facing the people I have to interview – it says 'Thank You For Not Smoking.'

LENNY: Ah yes, Chekhov . . . or was it Ibsen?

MALCOLM: It's manners, actually. Good manners.

(MALCOLM *turns away.*)

LENNY: Never heard of him . . . I have a sign in my office – facing the inevitable tray of contaminated custard creams – it says 'The things that are going to happen have already happened.' T. S. Eliot. I don't know what it meant to him, and it's a bit too late to ask him, but I know what it means to me.

RITCHIE: He reads the *Guardian.*

MALCOLM: Huh, I should have known. One of those windy little CND wets who said we should have given away the Falklands without a fight.

LENNY: Yeah, all right, but there won't be any fighting when the big one comes, tit-brain. We'll just get killed.

MALCOLM: You know nothing.

LENNY: And you do? And who are you when you're at

home? Apart from some lunatic looking for a bin and carrying a handbag.

MALCOLM: Take it from me, I know what I'm talking about, don't you worry.

LENNY: But I am worried – if you really do know what you're talking about – and you behave like you do – God help the rest of us!

MALCOLM: Has he been like this all afternoon?

RITCHIE: (*Eagerly*) Worse.

LENNY: No, go on. Tell me what you do, let me know how important you are. At least *try* and impress me, I can be quite easily impressed, Jaffa Cakes can impress me in certain moods.

MALCOLM: The man's mad.

LENNY: Correct. Tell me about your tie, go on, tell me. I think I know already, but tell me anyway.

MALCOLM: Territorial Army.

LENNY: That's my boy! The Territorial Army. (*Parade ground noises.*) Mop-heads for machine guns and bin lids for shields. 'We'll fight them on the beaches.' Yeah, when the Cruise missiles come we'll throw pebbles at them.

MALCOLM: Do you practise being offensive, or does it just come naturally?

LENNY: Nah, it took me years of study – I watched him.

RITCHIE: I'm telling you – I haven't hit anyone in years – but you – you're asking for it, you really are.

MALCOLM: And put that damned cigarette out!

(*Silence. And then the* NURSE *moves across the corridor from stage right to left.* MALCOLM *sees the* NURSE, *goes to follow him.*)

Nurse . . .

(*He passes* LENNY.)

LENNY: Ooh! Sneaky Poos!

THE PREPARATION ROOM

As the NURSE *approaches the curtained-off bed,* MALCOLM *enters.*

MALCOLM: Nurse, er can I have a few words with you?
NURSE: I'll be back directly.
MALCOLM: No, it's er in private. In confidence. I meant to mention it before, but I . . . I understand that a general anaesthetic is available . . .
NURSE: (*With just the slightest amusement*) With a vasectomy?
MALCOLM: Yes.
NURSE: At an extra cost, of course.
MALCOLM: Of course. (*No reply.*) So I can have a general anaesthetic, then?
NURSE: It's only a minor operation, you know. No more than three to five min—
MALCOLM: The problem is that my pain threshold is extremely low, my dentist told me, it's er purely physical.
NURSE: Pain often is.
MALCOLM: Er yes . . . right good, thank you.
(*The* NURSE *has moved towards the door.* MALCOLM *lingers slightly.*)
NURSE: If you'll come into the Waiting Room now, Mr Thomas . . . Oh, by the way, you haven't seen your wife recently by any chance, have you?
MALCOLM: I er a erm . . . my wife?
NURSE: Yes, she seems to be falling down again, sir. (*He takes* MALCOLM *out of the Preparation Room*) This way . . .

THE WAITING ROOM
MALCOLM *is still fumbling for words as he re-enters with the* NURSE.
MALCOLM: . . . Are you, I mean is it, are you sure?
NURSE: Oh yes. (*Turns to* LENNY.) Mr Anderson. Have you seen a woman wandering about?
(LENNY *looks at* MALCOLM *pointedly.*)
LENNY: Hah hah! Of course – Moriarty, the Master of Disguise! Revealed at last! (*To* RITCHIE) Another case solved, Watson.

(MALCOLM *is speechless. The* NURSE *is amused.*)

NURSE: What about you, Mr Burrows? Have you seen a young woman?

RITCHIE: Well, this bit of flesh popped her head around the door about ten minutes ago. A right little raver she looked and all. (*Begins now to address* MALCOLM.) You know the kind . . . auburn hair, come-to-bed eyes, nice tight arse on her, and the kind of . . .

(RITCHIE *suddenly realizes as* MALCOLM *stares malignantly at him.* RITCHIE *promptly gives* MALCOLM *his handbag back.*)

. . . generally speaking, seemed a very charming woman. She went that way.

(RITCHIE *points in the general direction of the corridor.* LENNY *grins broadly.* RITCHIE *glares at him.*)

MALCOLM: Er that's er . . . possibly it's er . . . my er wife was here, hence the er . . . (*Indicates the handbag.*) . . . but er she er I'm certain she went home . . . (*He looks at the* NURSE *and then at* LENNY. *Both shake their heads sadly.*) . . . That way? . . . (*He points stage left.* LENNY *points the opposite way.*) Well, I'll er . . . (*Gets to the doors.*) . . . just check . . . just in . . . just to make sure . . . in the unlikely . . .

(*The* NURSE *grins quietly and slowly approaches* LENNY *as* LENNY *sits, sideways, away from him, enjoying* RITCHIE'*s face.*)

NURSE: . . . Mr Anderson, please.

(RITCHIE *laughs sadistically.*)

LENNY: This it then, is it?

NURSE: Afraid so. I'm surprised you're still here, as a matter of fact.

LENNY: It was the company that kept me. Such vibrant wit and intellectual debate. (*Turns to* RITCHIE *as he approaches the door.*) But really, Big Jobs, it was your come-to-bed eyes . . .

RITCHIE: I hope the knife slips, I really do.

(*The* NURSE *has already gone.* LENNY *follows him out.*)

RITCHIE: Dick-head.

CORRIDOR AND WAITING ROOM

The old man, GEORGE, *and the younger woman* JEAN, *re-enter. Approach the waiting room.*

GEORGE: Ey-up lad, can you tell me where gents' toilet is?

RITCHIE: Down the corridor. First left.

GEORGE: Ta. C'mon, Jean.

THE PREPARATION ROOM

The NURSE *and* LENNY *enter.*

NURSE: . . . If you would remove all your clothing, please, Mr Anderson, there's a dressing gown there for you . . . really, it's nothing to worry about.

LENNY: Does it, I mean, will it hurt? At all?

NURSE: No, I won't feel a thing.

(NURSE *smiles genuinely. Goes out and off stage right.* LENNY *leans against the door. He then picks up the plastic clothes basket and goes past the bed towards the table and chair.* LENNY *puts the basket down, takes off his jacket and his jumper, then his shirt, dropping them into the basket. Talking all the way.*)

LENNY: . . . All right, all right . . . right . . . OK . . . well you're here . . . as is fairly bloody obvious . . . but you've done well . . . keep going, keep going . . . it's not as if you haven't suffered pain before . . . real pain . . . (*Half laughs.*) . . . the irony, bloody Big Jobs of all people . . . you've come a long way, Lenny . . . the spotty little sod with a slight squint went the way of all adolescents a long time ago . . . huh, anyone throws sand in your face now, they get battered to death with two tonne of chocolate digestives . . .

(LENNY *stops. He is in his trousers, shoes and socks. Goes across to the chair that has its back turned to the curtained-off bed. As he sits down, we see* DOREEN *peep out. She will become more adventurous and fascinated as he continues talking, and she will find a time to just sit on the edge of the bed behind him, oblivious to everything except what* LENNY *is saying.* LENNY *flips off his shoes as he starts talking again. Drops them in the basket. At no time does he actually address the audience. He is still behind the fourth wall.*)

Ladies and gentlemen . . . ladies and . . . (*He bends down to take his socks off.*) . . . gentlemen . . . (*Sniffs his socks.*) . . . ladies and gentlemen, my feet stink . . . (*He stands.*) . . . ladies and gentlemen, you see before you . . .

(*He undoes his trousers, then reaches over and pours a drink from the jug into the glass on the table. Almost takes a sip, but then puts the glass down and lets his trousers drop.*)

. . . you see before you a man caught with his trousers down . . . not a pretty sight . . .

(LENNY *then drinks deeply from the glass. Continues.*)

. . . but ladies and gentlemen, Ieeeeeeeeh!

(*He reacts to the vodka. Holds his chest and his stomach. Looks at the jug in amazement. Sniffs it, dips it, sips at the glass again. Then throws the rest of the vodka down himself. Pours himself a very stiff one. And enjoys it. Staggers and slurs for a second or two.*)

. . . but ladies and gentlemen . . . (*Steps out of his trousers.*) . . . ladies and gentlemen, I offer you this thought . . . I am your almost common man.

(*He takes his underpants off, drops them into the basket. We see he has cut himself shaving. There is a piece of tissue placed above his penis.*)

. . . Your naked ape . . . no, that's Big Jobs, he can do that one . . .

(*He looks down at himself, pulls the tissue off. Winces. Then he picks up his basket. Is about to move towards the dressing gowns on the hooks but doesn't.*)

I am your average Oxbridge scientist well versed in plutonium and working in a biscuit factory.

(*He puts the basket down at the side of the table.*)

I am a man of average total insecurity, well hidden with such a flair for words that he has recently been described as 'that clever twat who thinks he knows everything'

. . . I am an average kind of husband with a wife, three children, a mortgage, a budget account, a cottage in Llangollen, and money in the bank . . . I should be nearly happy, but I'm not . . . I could be nearly crazy, and I think I nearly am . . . this is the only life I will ever have, and I would like to believe that I'm less than half-way through it . . . but I don't . . . Jesus Christ, how can I when things are happening – *have happened* – that seem to indicate that I won't . . .

(*He goes down on his haunches. Whispers.*)

. . . and look, Monica, I want you to know, I want you to know the real reason why I am having this vasectomy, it's because there seems no point in creating and fathering a life and a future if there is no life in the future . . . and that is why I am self-employed in killing my life and its potential . . . and so, basically, at the moment, for the time being, I am alive and . . . well I'm having a breakdown in Britain in the eighties, and I want you to know – *and you'd better believe me – I AM FUCKING TERRIFIED!*

(*Silence. He falls to his knees, back turned to* DOREEN, *huddled into himself, his elbows drawn up. A foetal position.*)

DOREEN: (*Whispers*) That was wonderful.

LENNY: Yes, it was quite goo—

(*He turns, terrified. Sees* DOREEN *as she stands and moves off the bed.* LENNY *looks around in panic. A brief chase to the door and the clothes,* DOREEN *cutting him off. He sees, grabs and puts the bedpan across his privates. He backs straight into the corner of the table. Jumps away from it, towards* DOREEN.)

Er hi! There. This is er somewhat . . .

(*He laughs nervously and then bangs back into the corner of the table again.*)

Ow! . . . Er were you listening to me then?

DOREEN: Yes. You were wonderful.

LENNY: Was I? (*Glances manically under his bedpan.*)

DOREEN: Oh, yes. How can I thank you?

LENNY: A simple goodbye will do fine. (*Indicates the door.*) Goodbye, auf Wiedersehen, kindly leave the room, thank you for listening to me, remember nothing I've said to you.

DOREEN: I'll never forget it.

LENNY: Whatever you want.

(LENNY *tries to head for the door.* DOREEN *cuts him off. He is near to the bed. Jumps on it and pulls the curtains across himself, almost like a toga.*)

Do you like me in curtains? I wear them quite often at home, whatever takes my fancy actually, curtains, tablecloths, the odd tea tow—

(DOREEN *grabs the curtain and pulls it away from him. He places the bedpan into position again.*)

Ow! Me curtains.

(*He sits on the bed. She sits with him. As they talk he moves sideways away. She follows him. He slides off the bed as they talk, bounces on to the floor, trying to look natural and comfortable, open-legged and bedpanned, sitting on the floor.*)

DOREEN: I'm going to surprise you.

LENNY: Again?

DOREEN: You won't be expecting this.

LENNY: No doubt I won't.

DOREEN: You'll think I'm crazy.

LENNY: I think I already do.

DOREEN: I want to ask you something.

LENNY: No, I'm not Jewish, it just hangs that way.

DOREEN: Listen to me.

LENNY: I wouldn't mind being Jewish, I'm not bothered. I'm not prejudiced against anyone, apart from Australians.

DOREEN: Listen . . .

LENNY: The one thing you can say about Australians, they've got the courage of their ancestors' convictions.

DOREEN: *Please listen to me.*

LENNY: I've been trying to drop that into a conversation

for years!

DOREEN: *LISTEN TO ME!*

(*She throws herself at, over and on* LENNY. *In the mêlée he loses his bedpan. He pushes her away and turns to the table. He gets behind it, picks up the two legs of the table nearest him and uses it like a shield around and below his private parts.* DOREEN *still advances.*)

LENNY: Yeah yeah, all right, I'll listen. All ears.

DOREEN: Don't laugh.

LENNY: It's unlikely.

DOREEN: Take me home and make love to me.

LENNY: (*Quietly*) Yahhhhhhhhhhh!

(LENNY *looks down at his table, lifts it slightly away from himself, looks even more horrified. Retreats.*)

Down boy . . . and I thought I had problems.

DOREEN: Take me home and make love to me . . .

LENNY: Ah well, thank you very much. That's very kind of you, but you see, it's a bit difficult. The wife will be there. She tends to notice such things. And the kids will scream, I know they will. Sorry. But I'd be a terrible disappointment to you.

DOREEN: You wouldn't.

LENNY: No I would really – believe me – I have all the usual male problems – my breath smells, I fart in bed, I come too early, or I don't come at all, sometimes I even come and no one notices . . . it took me six years to find my wife's clitoris. It did. I looked everywhere, but . . .

(DOREEN *tries to get close to him. He jerks away.*)

No, please don't touch me, you see, I think I might be secretly gay, I buy all my clothes from Chelsea Girl, I vote Liberal, I'm a Barry Manilow fan!

DOREEN: I'm not talking about sex – I'm talking about two people giving each other love and warmth, helping each other.

LENNY: *I can hardly help myself. How can I help you?*

DOREEN: I'm scared. *I am so scared!*

LENNY: Don't be scared – laugh about it. You want a laugh?

There you are.

(*He drops his table and flashes her wildly. She does not react. He does it again, this time slower.*)

Look at that – driven many a woman to laughter, that has . . .

(*She half turns away from him. Speaks finally with a mixture of rage and tears.*)

DOREEN: I'm drinking myself silly, I'm so scared. And I'm so scared I can't get drunk any more. Not drunk enough anyway. I know what you're doing – I do it too – I try and hide it with ridicule and contempt and 'You're not going to get near me', but what I *feel* and what I *see* . . . and never get the chance to tell anyone . . . I see everything that in my own immature ridiculous way . . . I believed was . . . sacred . . . disappearing and turning to dust.

(LENNY, *without realizing, lets the table rest on the floor. Speaks in a whisper almost to himself*)

LENNY: . . . like decency and tolerance and common sense and peace in our time . . .

(*As* DOREEN *continues, he kneels behind the table, so that she can only see his head and shoulders.*)

DOREEN: Have you never sat there at night by your children's bedside, seen them snuggled up and lost in dreams, slobbering on their pillows, mumbling your name . . . have you never sat there and cried at the thought of the horror that lies ahead?

(LENNY *holds the legs of the table and butts the table top. Then butts it again. And again.*)

(*Evenly*) That's what I've been doing for the last three days . . . and nights, while my husband has been . . . away . . . (*She smiles grimly.*) . . . and instead of listening to his nightmares, I lived through them . . . I brought my children into bed with me. And sat there waiting . . .

LENNY: Don't talk like that.

DOREEN: (*With far less emphasis than before*) Take me away

somewhere, your cottage in Llangollen, anywhere, let's do it, let go now.

LENNY: No chance. The last time I made love, I kept thinking of Ronald Reagan.

(*Pause. He stands.*)

DOREEN: But what is there left? *What can we do?*

(*This time she lets him go past her. He leaves the table upturned and puts on a dressing gown as he talks.*)

LENNY: Pray? Join the TA? Built a fall-out shelter? Have a vasectomy? March for peace? Buy a machine gun? Collect sleeping tablets so when the time comes. . . ?

DOREEN: *NO!*

LENNY: Yes, we have to do something . . . but going to Llangollen isn't the answer . . . (*He kneels at her side.*) . . . Of course I want to do something, I desperately want to do something, but I'm not the stuff of dreams or leaders . . . not until I'm pushed so hard it's a matter of survival . . . or revenge. We all let that slip away. Fifteen years ago in what we thought were liberal times. And what terrifies me is that soon there may only be revenge left (*Very quietly*) Like a bomb in a briefcase.

DOREEN: A bomb in a what?

LENNY: . . . When I was sixteen two boys in our school tried to murder another boy. It was a serious attempt. I was . . . one of those two boys. And the boy we tried to murder is sitting in the Waiting Room.

DOREEN: The er . . .

LENNY: Stocky one. Yes. Big Jobs Burrows. 'Monster' for short.

DOREEN: But why?

LENNY: (*Sighs.*) It was like Blackpool. (*She looks puzzled at him.*) You know – the last resort. Or so it seemed at the time. He made our lives hell – we decided to send him there. (*Snorts.*) Yeah . . . made this bomb in the old shed at the bottom of my mate's garden. And when we'd made it, he took it into school . . . only he never got there. He went around and around on the bus just sitting there with the bomb in his bag almost waiting for it to go off.

DOREEN: Did it?

LENNY: Course it bloody well did. When I make a bomb, it goes off . . . He sort of cracked up on the bus, realizing what he was doing – while I cracked up waiting for him at the school gates ready to defuse the thing . . . I think we both cracked up weeks before actually, but . . . but when things get so terrible that you lose all reason, when nothing is left that is worth having, when everything good has been taken away from you, when all other alternatives have gone . . . you're left with revenge. Amen.

DOREEN: But what good will that be? Revenge'll be too late when we're all dead.

LENNY: No, it won't. There is a way. It's known in football terms as 'retaliate first' . . . (*He breaks the mood quickly.*) I don't even know what your name is.

DOREEN: . . . Clarissa.

LENNY: Come again.

DOREEN: Doreen.

LENNY: Thanks anyway . . . Doreen. Thanks for the offer.

DOREEN: Do you get many?

LENNY: None like that. (*Smiles.*) None at all really.

(*They both smile.* LENNY *picks up the vodka jug. Looks at it, then looks at her. Points to the jug.*)

LENNY: You er. . . ? Mmmmm?

DOREEN: Yes.

(*They both sit down, moving the chairs together. He offers her the jug.*)

LENNY: Yes?

DOREEN: Why not. (*She takes the jug and drinks.*)

LENNY: I don't drink much. Never did. Got scared off it, actually.

DOREEN: Why, what happened?

LENNY: Oh, it was my best mate at school, yeah, terrible, always was unlucky – dropped dead drinking a can of

Long Life.

(*He drinks from the jug, glances at her as he waits for the penny to drop. She laughs. He offers the jug back to her. She drinks heavily again.*)

DOREEN: I'm not so think as you drunk I am. (*She giggles.*)

LENNY: Oh good. (*He glances behind them towards the door.*) . . . Someone's going to come for us soon . . .

DOREEN: To take us away.

(*They look at each other. Move forward off their chairs together, to sit on the floor.*)

LENNY:
DOREEN: } 'They're coming to take us away, hah hah!'

LENNY: . . . Do you want to know something?

DOREEN: Yes.

LENNY: This man went to see his doctor, four o'clock in the afternoon. The doctor examined him, said 'Sorry to tell you this, my man, but you've only got twelve hours to live.' 'How many hours?' 'Twelve.' 'Jesus,' he said. Ran out the surgery, down to the post office, took out every penny he had, straight to the pub, saw all his mates, said, 'Come on, boys, a night to remember, I've got twelve hours left to live, the drinks are on me.' And they drank and they drank and they drank, and at closing time they went to a club in town and they drank and drank again. And it came to two o'clock in the morning and they got thrown out on to the street, and the man with twelve hours left to live said, 'It's all right, fellers, I've got a stack of booze at home, let's go.' And one of the others said, 'Nah, we've had enough.' And all the others agreed, and the man with twelve hours to live said, 'Ah, but why? Come on, boys, please!' And his friend said . . . 'It's all right for you, we've got to get up for work in the morning.'

(DOREEN *laughs.*)

DOREEN: That's terrible . . .

LENNY: Yeah. (*He takes the jug from her and drinks.*) Good health.

(*He passes the jug over. She drinks.*)

DOREEN: Yeah. Good health. All the best.

LENNY: Oh yes.

DOREEN: The very best.

LENNY: (*Taking* DOREEN*'s hand starts to sing, mock romantically.*) 'Take my hand, I'm a stranger in Paradise. Lost in a wonderland. A stranger in Paradise.'

(*The lights fade down on them. An actual recording of 'Strangers in Paradise' fades up as the house lights come up.*)

ACT TWO

Fifteen minutes later.

The John Lennon version of 'Stand By Me' precedes the start of Act Two. It is playing at the blackout, then fades slowly out as the action begins.

The lights fade up. And we see what DOREEN *and* LENNY *and the past quarter of an hour have done to the furniture.*

LENNY *is lying with his back against the table, turned on its side. The umbrella is open and perched above him, as if sheltering him from the sun.* DOREEN *has turned a chair over, taken a pillow from the bed, and lies against the chair and the pillow. They are both spreadeagled. And the jug is lying on its side. Very empty.*

LENNY *examines the jug on the off chance of a miracle, then surveys the room. Looks at* DOREEN.

LENNY: Are you . . . thinking of . . . staying here?

DOREEN: (*Tired*) No . . . I don't know.

LENNY: I wouldn't if I were you. Not only are they looking for you, but the next one in here is Big Jobs Burrows. And he really will make you scared. He thinks radioactive is . . . a wireless . . . that works.

DOREEN: I could go home. I suppose. Lend me £4.12p.

LENNY: You must live a long way away. Half a bottle away?

(DOREEN *shakes her head. Hesitates for a second or so.* LENNY *stands up, with a little difficulty. Picks up the umbrella. Begins to move towards the doorway. At the side of the door is the basket with his clothes in.*)

'I'm singing in the rain' . . .

(*He throws the umbrella on the bed, or on a hook.* DOREEN *follows him.*)

DOREEN: Lenny, there's only one thing I haven't told you. It's about my husband.

LENNY: Oh no, come on . . .

DOREEN: You know what my husband does?

LENNY: I don't know – he's in the TA – that's all I know. That's all I want to know.

DOREEN: He's the chief executive of the county council.

LENNY: Yes, well, I'm suitably impressed, I'll never pay another rate demand, but . . .

DOREEN: Absolute power of life and death.

LENNY: I don't take my rate demands that seriously.

(*We see the* NURSE *walk down the corridor from stage right to left.*)

DOREEN: I'm not talking about *now*. Just let me tell you. I'm talking about in the event of a . . .

(*The Preparation Room door opens. And the* NURSE *knocks* DOREEN *into* LENNY *as he opens the door.* LENNY *puts his arms around her instinctively.*)

NURSE: Mr Anderson . . . oh.

(*The* NURSE *can hardly take in the state of the room,* DOREEN *being there in* LENNY*'s arms.*)

. . . er Mrs Thomas? It is Mrs Thomas, isn't it?

DOREEN: For the time being. Lenny . . .

NURSE: There seems to be some misunderstanding, Mrs Thomas, your husband is looking for you.

DOREEN: That's the misunderstanding. You see, I'm not looking for him. Lenny, you have no idea what he does. And what he will do.

(LENNY *is just trying to get out of the corner by the open door. The* NURSE *tries to intervene.*)

NURSE: Mrs Thomas.

DOREEN: And what kind of suit he carries in his suitcase when he goes away.

LENNY: To be honest, I'm more concerned about . . .

(LENNY *points in the direction of the Operating Theatre.*)

NURSE: Mrs Thomas, *please*.

DOREEN: Shall I show you. Shall I?

LENNY: Take me away, nurse. I'm all yours.

(*The* NURSE *tries to take hold of* DOREEN*'s arm, and guide her towards the open doorway.*)

DOREEN: I can, you know. I can show you exactly what he will be wearing . . .

(*The* NURSE *manages to move her towards the door. And*

MALCOLM *hurries past with handbag and frown.*
MALCOLM *double-takes.*)

MALCOLM: *Doreen!* (*Then gently*) Doreen. I've been looking for you everywhere.
(MALCOLM *then takes in the* NURSE *and* LENNY *and the room. Looks back at* LENNY.)
Whatever are you doing here?

DOREEN: I was hoping to go to Llangollen.
(LENNY *coughs and splutters suddenly. Nearly chokes.*)

MALCOLM: Llangollen?

NURSE: All right, Mr Anderson?

LENNY: Oh yes, fine, just the start of a coronary . . .

MALCOLM: *I'll* look after the situation now, nurse. Thank you. (*He takes hold of* DOREEN*'s arm.*) I'll just – Doreen, if you'll come with me, we'll . . .

NURSE: Would you stay in the Waiting Room, please, Mr Thomas.

MALCOLM: I was er just erm . . . (*Reaches the corridor, pulling* DOREEN, *and points the other way. Towards London.*)

NURSE: No, I'd like you in the Waiting Room at this time, I'll be . . . needing you shortly.

MALCOLM: I'd only be . . . (*Looks at his watch.*)

DOREEN: (*Now taking hold of* his *arm.*) Oh come on, darling. Let's wait in the Waiting Room, like you wanted to, remember?
(DOREEN, *as she speaks, leads the way strongly towards the Waiting Room.* MALCOLM *tries to stop at one point but is jerked forward by* DOREEN.)

NURSE: Are you fit?

LENNY: Funnily enough, I was just about to have one.
(LENNY *picks up his basket and follows the* NURSE *as they go towards stage right, past the corridor.*)

THE WAITING ROOM

DOREEN *and* MALCOLM *enter.* RITCHIE *has just inhaled on a cigarette as they enter. Stubs it out and backheels it fast. Holds his breath, looks at* MALCOLM *and* DOREEN. *Half waves, half wafts the smoke away from him. Smiles without opening his mouth.*

As this happens, we see the NURSE *walk across. We see* LENNY *follow him. We see* MALCOLM *looking away,* DOREEN *looking over his shoulder towards the corridor. And* LENNY *lifts his dressing gown up and shows his backside to* DOREEN, *who giggles. And* MALCOLM *turns around and misses it all as* LENNY *goes.* MALCOLM *moves* DOREEN *towards the corner by the phone.* RITCHIE *exhales smoke madly.*

MALCOLM: (*Between clenched teeth and lips*) I want to see you.

DOREEN: You're looking at me now, sweetness.

(MALCOLM *forces* DOREEN *to sit down. She sits with a bump into the chair.* RITCHIE *looks across with the noise.* MALCOLM *is sitting smiling out, in a fashion.*)

RITCHIE: Hello again!

DOREEN: Why, hello . . .

(MALCOLM *applies pressure to her hand. They struggle, silently.*)

RITCHIE: You found each other then, hey?

MALCOLM: *Yes.*

RITCHIE: (*Approaching*) I'm sorry, you did say your name, but I never quite caught it . . .

DOREEN: He never threw it anywhere, did you, darling?

MALCOLM: Thomas.

RITCHIE: Mine's Ritchie. You don't mind if I call you 'Tom', Tom? (*Laughs.*) 'Tom-Tom!'

MALCOLM: (*Murderously*) Thomas is my second name.

RITCHIE: Ah. Hahhhhhhh . . .

(*Failed again. But he tries, again.*)

RITCHIE: Well, there you go, hey-ho . . . here we are, having a . . . (*Thinks better of it.*) . . . funny isn't it, how things always come, you know, they seem to be weeks away, and then suddenly they're here . . .

DOREEN: (*Sweetly*) I think it's got something to do with the passage of time.

RITCHIE: Yes! . . . yes . . .

(*Poor* RITCHIE *is left standing there. Claps his hands*

together, then removes himself. Sits down again.)

THE OPERATING THEATRE

The swing doors crash open. The SURGEON *enters, dressed in elegant 'civvies'. Followed by the* NURSE.

SURGEON: Nice to see you're still here . . .

NURSE: Well, till five o'clock at least. (*No reaction.*) You been out?

SURGEON: Yes, I've been stopping strangers in the street – 'Excuse me, have you got nursing qualifications?'

NURSE: Ah, dressed to kill, as it were? (*She withers him.*) All right, all right.

SURGEON: John, the patient who needs the abortion is here.

NURSE: Who *wants* the abortion.

SURGEON: She needs it. I've just seen her.

NURSE: So?

SURGEON: So, she is fifteen years old, she doesn't want the child, she hardly knew the father and doesn't know him any more, she's been hiding the pregnancy for five months, and if she waits much longer she will have to have the child.
(*Silence.*)
SHE WILL HAVE TO HAVE THE CHILD.

NURSE: Listen, most of our abortions are middle-class ladies with money who don't want the inconvenience.

SURGEON: Right – I'm going to get someone, I don't care who I get, Attila the Hun'll do, but I'm going to do it. (*She moves away.*) I'm going to try again . . .

NURSE: (*At the door, pointing off*) What about him?

SURGEON: He can wait . . .

LENNY: (*Off and plaintively*) I don't like waiting . . .

THE WAITING ROOM

DOREEN: Malcolm . . . Malcolm . . . coooooooey, Malcolm!

MALCOLM: (*Facing out*) What?

DOREEN: I'm going now.

MALCOLM: Not till you tell me just what has been going on.

DOREEN: Oh well, in that case I'm definitely going.
MALCOLM: You're not.
DOREEN: I am.
MALCOLM: No you're not.
DOREEN: Oh yes I am, oh no you're not, oh yes I am.
MALCOLM: *Doreen.*
DOREEN: Ooooooh look, angel, *Ideal Home.*

(She points towards the magazines on the coffee table. Stands up and goes over to the table. MALCOLM *jumps up and follows her. They stand facing front pretending to peruse a magazine each.* MALCOLM *whispers harshly, aware of* RITCHIE *and, as always, trying to keep a public face on things.)*

MALCOLM: I am going to make you pay for this, Doreen.
DOREEN: I can afford it. Your magazine's upside down, darling.
MALCOLM: You've made an absolute fool out of me.
DOREEN: Cheap at twice the price then, wasn't it? . . .

*(*MALCOLM *throws the magazine down. Grabs hold of* DOREEN*'s arm. Pulls her towards the door. And the door opens as the* NURSE *enters.* MALCOLM *does an about-face and drags* DOREEN *with him.)*

NURSE: . . . Mr Burrows.

(The NURSE *smiles wickedly.* RITCHIE *is reluctant to leave the room. Finally stands and goes towards the door, with his briefcase.)*

RITCHIE: Oh well . . . see you then.
DOREEN: I hope so. Bye . . . Big Jobs.

*(*RITCHIE *looks amazed and then at* DOREEN. MALCOLM *looks amazed and then at* DOREEN. *The* NURSE *escorts* RITCHIE *out as* RITCHIE *looks over his shoulder.* MALCOLM *grabs* DOREEN *and marches her towards the door.* MALCOLM *aims stage left,* DOREEN *goes stage right.* MALCOLM *hurries after her.)*

THE PREPARATION ROOM

The NURSE *and* RITCHIE *enter. As* RITCHIE *looks amazed at the way* DOREEN *and* LENNY *have left the room, the* NURSE *sets about tidying it.*

NURSE: . . . If you would take your clothes off, Mr Burrows, your dressing gown is over there.

RITCHIE: . . . What happens next? After I take off my. . . ?

NURSE: Not a lot. I come back and take you down to the theatre, but I wouldn't rush. We have a slight delay.

RITCHIE: Will it . . . will it hurt much?

NURSE: No, I won't feel a thing. (*Laughs, smacks* RITCHIE *on the shoulder.*) There's nothing to it, really.

(*The* NURSE *exits, goes stage right.* RITCHIE *then begins to get undressed behind the curtained part of the bed.*)

THE WAITING ROOM

As the NURSE *leaves the Preparation Room and moves across,* MALCOLM *and* DOREEN *re-enter from stage right.* MALCOLM *turns sharp right into the Waiting Room with* DOREEN, *watches the* NURSE *go across. Half waves to him.* DOREEN *moves down to sit on a chair.* MALCOLM *advances on her finally.*

MALCOLM: If I was a different kind of man, I would batter you.

DOREEN: If you were a different kind of man, darling, you wouldn't have to.

(*Whereupon he promptly hits her, across the head, to the astonishment of both.*)

MALCOLM: . . . I . . . I'm sorry, I . . . I didn't mean to do that.

DOREEN: What a perfect excuse, one I'm sure the Americans and Russians are already preparing. 'Oops, sorry Romania.'

MALCOLM: *SHUT UP! SHUT UP! SHUT UP!* You always bring it back to that, don't you. Always, always, the same target, it always ends up there!

DOREEN: Like a homing missile.

MALCOLM: It isn't going to happen. It isn't. It can't happen. Nobody will allow it to happen. That's what I've got a small part in doing – and damn you, I'm doing it because

I want to do it – *I want to do it* – because I know I'm right – I'm looking after all of us – if we don't look after ourselves, who will?

DOREEN: Oh, absolutely, sweetheart. 'It's all right for you, we've got to get up for work in the morning.'

MALCOLM: What?

DOREEN: Nothing.

MALCOLM: Look, the ultimate weapon is the ultimate cure – don't you understand that – we're making sure it will never be used!

DOREEN: Every ultimate weapon since the bow and arrow has been used, Malcolm. Why not this one?

MALCOLM: It will never be used – that's what it's there for.

DOREEN: Ah, I see. Hiroshima was just a rumour.

MALCOLM: It will never be used *again*.

DOREEN: Something like your own weapon, angel?

(MALCOLM *goes down on his knees, makes weak flailing actions to hit* DOREEN, *like a child. She continues talking as he tries to hit her.*)

MALCOLM: Oh you bastard, you bitch, you're killing me. (*She laughs.*) . . . Doreen, *Doreen*, I've given you everything you've ever wanted or even remotely needed, whatever it was that I did – I've done nothing to deserve this!

DOREEN: You're the chief executive of the county council and you're a major in the TA.

MALCOLM: Oh no . . . no . . . I've explained . . .

DOREEN: And you haven't got a cottage in Llangollen, and you talk to yourself in your sleep, and you don't know that your dreams have turned into nightmares, and you aren't scared. That's what I really despise about you, Malcolm. You're not scared. But why should you be scared, with your special issue suit in your secret suitcase.

(MALCOLM *grabs hold of* DOREEN, *pushes and almost strangles her on to the floor. He is above her as they struggle furiously. Enter a very* OLD MAN. *Behind him is his* WIFE.

She is in her mid-thirties. As we have seen earlier, both are classically and richly dressed in a casual way. The very OLD MAN *speaks in fairly broad dialect. He also radiates vigour and health and Jehovah-like joy of life. His* WIFE *treats him with a mixture of irony and affection.*)

GEORGE: (*Outside the doors*) This must be it, Jean, No Man's Land!

(*He enters, followed by* JEAN, *and sees* MALCOLM *and* DOREEN *as they disentangle.*)

Areet, cock! Lost something, have thee?

(MALCOLM *is crawling towards the coffee table for cover.* DOREEN *turns on to her side and begins to stand up.*)

MALCOLM: Hah! Er, yes, lost er . . . contact lenses! Yes . . .

GEORGE: What?

MALCOLM: (*Shouts*) *Contact lenses!* Lost them. One of them. One. Contact lens. My wife.

DOREEN: It was apparently in my mouth . . .

GEORGE: The first wife wore contact lenses, aye, waste of soddin' time, still couldn't see a soddin' thing . . . Don't just stand there, Jean, sit down girl, take the weight off your mind . . .

(DOREEN *moves towards a chair, stage left. Nearest to the door.* JEAN *sits alongside her.* MALCOLM *sits stage right, furthest away from* DOREEN. *Both are in a state of shock for some time.*)

She were my physiotherapist, this one, you know, aye – when I proposed to her, I went down on bended knee and showed her my bank book.

JEAN: He's got a lovely bank book.

GEORGE: No, she did, she married me for my money. That's right isn't it, woman?

JEAN: Absolutely.

GEORGE: Thought she'd have two years of Phyllosan and Horlicks, high blood pressure and dizzy spells and then off I'd soddin' pop, leavin' her a fortune.

JEAN: 'Not soddin' likely.'

GEORGE: Not soddin' likely.

JEAN: 'Bugger that for a lark.'

GEORGE: Bugger that for a lark. *What?* (JEAN *smiles and shakes her head.*) I didn't spend forty years running the largest waste disposal firm in Lancashire, just to dispose of myself when I'd got the time to enjoy it. Sod that for a game of arrows!

(GEORGE *cheerfully approaches* MALCOLM. *Goes to sit alongside him, then brings his chair around at right angles to* MALCOLM, *trapping him in. He slaps* MALCOLM*'s knee exuberantly.* MALCOLM *looks down at his knee, stares out front.*)

How old d'you reckon I am, hey? How old? Go on. Guess – how old d'you think I am?

MALCOLM: Oh Christ . . .

GEORGE: What? *What?*

(MALCOLM *shakes his head.*)

Seventy-seven. Aye. *Seventy soddin' seven.* Last August.

MALCOLM: (*Finally and flatly*) That's . . . that's . . . wonderful.

GEORGE: Aye and I've never had so much 'fun' in all me soddin' life! Know what I mean, hey? Hey? (*Smacks* MALCOLM*'s knee again.*) Ask her if you don't believe me.

(*No reply from* MALCOLM.)

Go ahead, ask her. Go on.

MALCOLM: Thank you, no.

GEORGE: *What?*

MALCOLM: Thank you, no, I'll take your sodd— . . . I'll take your word for it.

(MALCOLM *grabs a magazine off the coffee table.*)

GEORGE: Jean, tell him. Go on, tell him. I exhaust you, don't I.

JEAN: Yes, you exhaust me.

GEORGE: Very good, Jean.

JEAN: My patience, mainly.

GEORGE: I've even got a motto for it, you know, a catch phrase – 'Sex for the Over-Sixties – Life before Death'.

Good hey? I give lectures on the subject for 'Help the Aged'. Oh aye yes, I don't mind admitting it.

(MALCOLM *has his head down, flicking wildly through a magazine.*)

And you know why, young man? (*Pause.*) Do you want to know why?

(MALCOLM *is trying not to answer or look.* GEORGE *reaches over and catches him in mid flick and rests his hand on Malcolm's magazine.*)

I'll tell thee why. My first wife, young man, my first wife. (*Shakes his head.*) Rationed, I was. Rationed. Once a month for forty years, with her teeth clenched, her eyes closed and the alarm set to go off after ten minutes. And no imagination whatsoever. None. Asked her once if she fancied felatio – she said she didn't like package holidays.

(DOREEN *laughs. Begins to take in* GEORGE *more.*)

. . . It got so in the end, when the soddin' month was up and the night'd come, I used to look at her putting the sodding alarm on and turn over and go to sleep. And then . . . and then, oh happy day . . . she died. September the eighth, 1972. No flowers, just mass cards and ration books. Aye . . . it wasn't long before I put myself in a Home. Not one of those council ones, mind, full of elderly riff-raff. No, a good home in Southport. Jean here was my physio.

MALCOLM: Well well well, very interesting.

(MALCOLM *begins to 'read' the magazine.* GEORGE *carefully removes it from his hands and drops it on the floor.*)

GEORGE: But, young man, the point I'm making, for your information, is this – when I was your age, I thought growing old was a process of farting by the fireplace, growing sterile and becoming senile. (*Shakes his head slowly.*) No.

MALCOLM: . . . No?

GEORGE: No. Not true at all. Not if you're lucky. Not if you don't want to, and not in my case. Not in Southport. I met my first liberated lady in Southport. She was sixty-eight . . . and she was just the first. Aye . . . night after night after soddin' night they were at it there. (*Sighs.*) It were like fasting for forty years and then being invited to a feast . . . the only trouble was their stamina didn't match their appetite. Aye, they kept dying on me. Bloody shame like, but not a bad way to go, better than being run over by a bus on a Pelican Crossing . . .

(*He sits back, momentarily contented.* MALCOLM *practically climbs over* GEORGE*'s legs, moves towards the door, signalling manically to* DOREEN *to follow him out into the corridor. She ignores him. He stands by the doors and the telephone.*)

DOREEN: (*Quietly*) Is all that true?

JEAN: Oh yes.

DOREEN: Amazing . . .

JEAN: Yes, he is . . . the only trouble is he waited till he was looking at death before he got angry and started to live – and that's too late, love.

DOREEN: Yes. (*She looks at* MALCOLM, *and his signals.*) *Yes.* It is.

GEORGE: Too bloody true it is! (*Looks around.*) What? (*No answer.*) . . . Aye, happiest days of my life. Till I married Jean here.

(*Galvanized again, he looks for* MALCOLM. *Stands and approaches him, getting his wallet out and producing a photograph.*)

See these? See?

MALCOLM: . . . Ah yes, grandchildren.

GEORGE: (*Rising*) Grandchildren, sir? Grandchildren my arse! They're ours. Why the bloody hell do you think I'm having a vasectomy? Because it's fashionable? By God, that's what I've been saying to you man – go out with a bang not a soddin' whimper! (*Points angrily at* MALCOLM.) Do you know the daftest words in the English language? Hey? Hey?

(MALCOLM *hurries away from him, towards the chairs.*

And GEORGE *follows.*)

MALCOLM: I can't take much more . . .

GEORGE: You don't know, do you? Hey? No? I'll tell you. It was that silly old twat, J. M. Barrie. 'Peter Pissin' Pan'. The man was mad. Know what he wrote – *'To die will be an awfully big adventure.' BALLS TO THAT!* Go hurtling down the hill, young man, it's better in the valley than you think, live life to the soddin' full and go screaming into the hereafter!

(GEORGE *finishes up with his fist held high. Seems at last to have run out of steam, until . . .*)

. . . I want to hang glide but she won't let me . . .

(GEORGE *approaches* JEAN, *sits with her.*)

. . . Aye well, you can stop pretending to listen to me now.

(*Silence.*)

THE OPERATING THEATRE

We hear the internal phone ringing. And ringing. And ringing. We see LENNY *pacing up and down outside. In the corridor.*

THE PREPARATION ROOM

We see RITCHIE *now undressed apart from his undies. We see him begin to fiddle with the blind that doesn't cover the Preparation Room window. He flips it down and it shoots up again. He tries again. And again it shoots up. This time he uses some force to keep it down. And pulls the blind away from the mooring. Tries to put it back up with no success. Looks around anxiously for somewhere to hide it. Finally sticks it beneath the bed sheets in the bed.*

THE OPERATING THEATRE

The phone still ringing. We see LENNY *peep into the room. He hesitates. Then enters, shielding his eyes from the operating table, and approaching the phone.* LENNY *goes to pick it up. And it stops.* LENNY *goes to turn away. Then looks back, sees the typewritten list of internal numbers above the phone. Looks quickly down it. Begins dialling.*

THE PREPARATION ROOM AND OPERATING THEATRE

RITCHIE *has just got rid of the broken blind. Moves away towards his dressing gown. The internal phone rings. He flinches and looks guiltily at the bed. Approaches the phone.*

RITCHIE: . . . Hello?

(LENNY *disguises his voice, and talks in the most reverential 'Vincent Price' funeral tones.*)

LENNY: Ah, good afternoon. Mr Burrows, I believe . . .

RITCHIE: Er yes?

LENNY: I wonder if you could be of some assistance to us, Mr Burrows, it's Craven's Funeral Services here, we have the exclusive contract for this clinic, would you mind giving us your measurements, please, you know, on the off chance . . .

(RITCHIE *leans heavily against the wall. Holds the phone away from himself in fear and then disbelief as* LENNY *continues.*)

. . . Would you say you were a normal coffin size, Mr Burrows? We offer a special reduction to those who can even if it's a tight squeeze, be classified as . . .

RITCHIE: It's you, isn't it! It's you. It is. I know it is. I'm going to . . . I'm . . . I will . . .

LENNY: *BIG JOBS!*

(LENNY *laughs richly over Ritchie's attempt to threaten him.* LENNY *puts the phone down and goes out, still shielding his eyes.* RITCHIE *throws the phone down and sits on the bed.*)

THE WAITING ROOM

MALCOLM *approaches* DOREEN. *Stands by her with a magazine. Speaks like a ventriloquist again. She responds as the dummy. He kneels down at her side, cutting off the view of* GEORGE *and his* WIFE.

MALCOLM: . . . Doreen . . . Doreen.

DOREEN: (*Moving her head from side to side*) Gottle of geer, gottle of geer?

MALCOLM: I'm going outside.

(*She collapses against his shoulder loosely.*)

GEORGE: *What?*

(MALCOLM *gives up. And the doors open and the* NURSE *enters.*)

NURSE: Mr Thomas, ple—

(*He sees* GEORGE. *Surprise registers, big but brief.*)

Mr Hill?

GEORGE: What?

NURSE: The Mr Hill for the vasectomy?

JEAN: Yes.

NURSE: Ah . . . fine. I'll be with you shortly. (*Ticks him off.*) This way, Mr Thomas . . .

(MALCOLM *stands, but not before* DOREEN. *She reaches the* NURSE *first.*)

DOREEN: I'll come with you, darling.

MALCOLM: *Doreen.*

DOREEN: That's all right, isn't it, nurse?

NURSE: It's entirely up to you and your husband.

DOREEN: Signed and sealed then. Lead the way, men.

(DOREEN *marches out, towards the Preparation Room.*)

MALCOLM: But . . .

GEORGE: *What?*

(MALCOLM *half stops to look at* GEORGE, *and then follows the* NURSE *who is following* DOREEN.)

JEAN: Nothing, George.

GEORGE: Yes, I know. Nothing. I feel like a soddin' Jehovah's Witness sometimes.

(JEAN *takes hold of his hand.*)

THE PREPARATION ROOM

As GEORGE *speaks in the Waiting Room,* DOREEN *sweeps into the Preparation Room, approaches* RITCHIE *on the bed. She sits next to him, closely.*

DOREEN: Hi . . .

RITCHIE: Hi!

(*Then the* NURSE *and* MALCOLM *come in and* RITCHIE

stands up quickly and moves away. He picks up his basket of clothes and gets to the door.)

NURSE: If you would get undressed, Mr Thomas, a dressing gown is over there for you. I'll be back when we're ready.

(*The* NURSE *goes out with* RITCHIE *and off stage right.* MALCOLM *looks at* DOREEN, *who is sitting on the bed, her head in her hands. He looks away, sees the water jug, goes to pour a drink, finds it is empty. Pushes it away. He begins to take off his jacket and his tie.*)

MALCOLM: Hangover?

DOREEN: *Headache.*

MALCOLM: Can you tell the difference these days?

DOREEN: It's a headache – these contact lenses, Malcolm.

(*He walks past her to get the clothes basket. She flops on to the bed. Looks puzzled, investigates and finds the broken blind. Offers it to* MALCOLM. *He takes it and then doesn't know what to do with it. He puts it on the table eventually and begins to get undressed.*)

MALCOLM: . . . What is happening to us? I'm sorry. I am sorry, Doreen.

DOREEN: You will be . . .

MALCOLM: Please. No more. Don't start again. Not now.

(*He begins to pile his clothes into the basket, which is near the end of the bed, and within grabbing range of* DOREEN. *She becomes aware of this as he talks. And he mainly talks with his back turned.*)

. . . Whatever you do, don't go to sleep, Doreen.

DOREEN: Oh I wouldn't miss this for the world . . .

MALCOLM: Look, why don't you . . . can I trust you to go home?

DOREEN: I didn't know you had red undies.

MALCOLM: They were white till you washed them with the serviettes.

DOREEN: Oh yes . . .

(*We see* DOREEN *rummaging quietly in his jacket pocket. She takes the key that the* NURSE *gave to* MALCOLM.)

MALCOLM: (*Turning and putting his trousers on the basket.*) All right, but whether I can trust you or not, I want you to go home, Doreen.

(DOREEN *lifts the basket up, swings off the bed.* MALCOLM *is sitting, back turned, about to take his socks off.*)

DOREEN: I'd much rather stay, I could tell you about it afterwards.

MALCOLM: You're so kind, but I'd rather you went home. Pass me my dressing gown, would you?

(DOREEN *is at the door with his basket. She realizes that she has left his dressing gown. Grabs it as well.*)

DOREEN: I've got other plans actually, darling.

(*He turns around, one sock on and one sock half off. He sees her smiling at the open door.*)

See you later.

(*She goes out and off stage left quickly. He runs for the door in his undies and half a sock. As he does so, the* ANAESTHETIST *walks across the corridor from right to left. And* MALCOLM *meets him just outside the doorway.*)

MALCOLM: Ahhhhhhh. Hello!

(MALCOLM *hustles back into the Preparation Room and slams the door. The* ANAESTHETIST *opens the door and looks at* MALCOLM *enquiringly.* MALCOLM *slams the door in his face. Storms to the bed and sits down, head in his hands.*)

THE OPERATING THEATRE

The SURGEON *sweeps in at great pace, her face mask already in place. The* NURSE *then brings* LENNY *in. He is wildly cheerful and swinging his jockstrap.*

LENNY: . . . Don't I get a trolley?

NURSE: No, you get the trolley afterwards. You'll need it then.

LENNY: Thanks . . . Ooops, just remembered. Spend a penny. Won't be long.

(LENNY *dodges around the operating table away from the* NURSE, *backs away from the* SURGEON *quickly and makes for the doors. Where the* NURSE *catches him.*)

NURSE: Come on, Mr Anderson, you went to the toilet yesterday, and we didn't see you again.

(*As both men get to the doors, they see* RITCHIE *peeping through one of the windows in the swing doors.* LENNY *opens the door.*)

LENNY: You can go first if you want, Big Jobs.

(*No answer as* RITCHIE *disappears from view. The* NURSE *leads* LENNY *away, towards the operating table.*)

NURSE: Dressing gown, please, Mr Anderson. Just lie down please.

(LENNY *sits on the operating table. The* SURGEON *has her back turned, preparing the instruments on the trolley.*)

LENNY: Good afternoon, doctor, we've never met before and I wish it had stayed that way . . .

(*The* SURGEON *turns, knife in hand, towards* LENNY.)

I had a knife once, I called it Stanley . . .

(*The* NURSE *takes Lenny's dressing gown off, takes his jockstrap and hangs it on the corner of the instrument trolley. He takes* LENNY*'s shoulders and makes him lie down.*)

Well, I've had a very pleasant time here, but I expect it's going to stop now . . .

(*As* LENNY *talks, the* SURGEON *advances upon* LENNY *with a bowl and a long handled brush. The* NURSE *takes hold of and moves* LENNY*'s penis to one side so that his testicles can be washed with the brush.*)

(*Hurtling up, looking at the* NURSE) Get off! (*And the* SURGEON *starts brushing his testicles*) *What are you doing?*

SURGEON: Would you lie down, please?

LENNY: Yes, cert— (*Goes to lie down. Comes up.*) Pardon!?

SURGEON: *Would you lie down please.*

(LENNY *jumps off the table, turns to the* NURSE. *And covers his privates.*)

LENNY: It's a woman.

SURGEON: What did you expect – a fucking labrador!

LENNY: (*Gets straight on the table.*) Sorry, yes, you're right, of course, man, woman, or Big Jobs, it doesn't matter.

(*And the* NURSE *approaches with a green body cover, which he drops around* LENNY*'s body. We see that there is a circular hole, approximately 9 in (23 cm) in circumference in the middle of the cloth. The* NURSE *arranges it so that* LENNY*'s privates protrude.* LENNY *stares at it.*)

I feel like a billiard table. (*He adopts the reverential snooker commentator's whisper:*) 'There're only two balls left on the table . . .' (*He looks up at the* SURGEON.) Are you sure you're not Hurricane Higgins?

(*The* SURGEON *picks up a hypodermic needle from a tray.* lenny *promptly sits up.*)

I'm sorry to trouble you, but I've changed my mind, yes, what else can I have for £45? I can probably go up to 60 – I won't tell anyone – I've got a wart under my arm that's been troubling me for some time, you could do that for me . . .

(*He grabs the body cover and moves it up his body, so that his head peeps out of the hole.*)

How about a face lift? Yes, I want a face lift – I've wanted one all along. I just didn't want anyone to know. Will you take payments in instalments?

NURSE: (*Laughing*) Just lie down, Mr Anderson.

SURGEON: (*Not laughing*) And *relax*.

LENNY: *Relax?* How can I relax when I think I've got Legionnaire's Disease? (*Sits up again.*) You didn't know that, did you? I only felt it coming on myself at lunchtime, sort of . . . like . . . you know . . .

SURGEON: *Yes?* (*Pause.*) You were about to describe the symptoms of Legionnaire's Disease.

LENNY: Ah, yes, well, basically – you die.

SURGEON: And that is not going to happen to you. Not here anyway.

(*She spurts a couple of drops of liquid out of the hypodermic needle.* LENNY *jumps.*)

LENNY: No er you see . . .

SURGEON: (*Forcefully*) Mr Anderson, I want you to lie back, lie still and relax. *Now.*

(LENNY *lies back, stiffly.*)
I said *relax.*
(LENNY'*s back arches up. The* NURSE *pushes him down.*)
Good. Now don't worry. I'm just going to give you a little prick.
(LENNY *rears up wildly. Puts his hands over his privates again. The* SURGEON *throws the hypodermic needle at the sink and turns away.*)

LENNY: I beg your pardon? What sort of a side effect is that? I mean, it's nothing to write home about as it is.

SURGEON: Get him out.
(LENNY *grabs the jockstrap hanging on the trolley.*)

LENNY: Don't worry, I'm going. (*Points to his private parts.*) You had a lucky escape there, my son . . .
(*The* NURSE *goes for Lenny's dressing gown. He quite clearly has enjoyed the mayhem that* LENNY *has caused for the last four days.* LENNY *meanwhile has got wildly muddled up in his jockstrap. He has missed the straps and taken the waistband up to his chest, and then got it back to front at the second attempt. He then puts it on his head.*)
Biggles to Algy. Biggles to Algy.

SURGEON: Are you normally this infantile?

LENNY: As often as possible. My kids keep asking me what I'm going to do when I grow up.
(*He smiles charmingly, to no avail. The* NURSE *puts the dressing gown on* LENNY, *and begins to escort him to the door.*)
I'm terribly sorry about this, doctor, if I could only make amends . . .

SURGEON: Go away.

LENNY: There is just something I'd like to do before I go, if you don't mind.

NURSE: (*As they approach the doors*) Go on . . .

LENNY: Thank you. AAAAAAAAGGGGGGGGGGGHHH-HHHHHHHHH!
(*The* SURGEON *drops her kidney bowl and instruments.* MALCOLM *sits up on the bed in the Preparation Room.*

GEORGE *jumps.* JEAN *goes to the doorway in the Waiting Room. And the* NURSE *manages to cut off the end of the scream, unfortunately producing a curious choking sound from* LENNY. *Then we hear a loud thump and a collision with furniture/trolley outside the Operating Theatre.* LENNY *glances through the swing doors.*)

Ah poor Big Jobs. He seems to have fainted.

(*The* NURSE *goes through the doorway. We perhaps see* RITCHIE*'s outstretched feet. The* SURGEON *marches to the doorway.* LENNY *smiles at her.*)

Oh dear, what a shame . . .

(LENNY *goes out to 'help'.*)

SURGEON: Get him a glass of water, Mr Gilbert . . . *NO*, I don't think we require your help, Mr Anderson . . .

(LENNY *appears at the door.*)

LENNY: (*Casually*) He never used to faint at school . . .

SURGEON: I do not suffer fools gladly, Mr Anderson, and I do not intend to suffer you at all.

LENNY: (*Leaning against the door*) Are you going to ask him if he wants a little prick?

SURGEON: *Go over there and stay there!*

LENNY: (*As he goes*) I've waited twenty years for this . . . I'm a scientist in a biscuit factory. I know about first aid. Have you tried kicking him, that usually wakes people up.

SURGEON: Mr Gilbert, bring the next patient in here, please. Keep him out of reach of that buffoon . . .

(*The* NURSE *brings a shaky and now openly scared* RITCHIE *into the Theatre.*)

RITCHIE: What happened?

NURSE: You fainted.

RITCHIE: No, what happened to him?

NURSE: Nothing. It was his idea of a joke.

(RITCHIE *turns away towards the doors.*)

RITCHIE: I'll bloody well kill him.

(*The* NURSE *easily stops him.*)

SURGEON: Please, don't kill him just yet. A death on the

premises is no good for our reputation . . .

NURSE: It depends how you define 'death'.

(*The* SURGEON *glares at the* NURSE. RITCHIE *gulps at them.*)

SURGEON: Now, nobody is rushing you, Mr . . . (*She glances at her watch.*)

NURSE: Burrows.

SURGEON: Mr Burrows. Nobody is rushing you, and you can do what you want with him as soon as you've gone out of the gates, you have my full approval. But for the moment, lie down and rest . . . are you prone to fainting?

RITCHIE: Only when I'm having a vasectomy. (*He tries to laugh.*)

SURGEON: Lie down. We won't do anything till you're ready.

(*The* NURSE *helps* RITCHIE *on to the table in his dressing gown. The* SURGEON *moves away, indicates the* NURSE *to follow.*)

John, how many more after him?

NURSE: Two.

SURGEON: Get the next one down. It's getting late.

NURSE: The next one wants a general.

SURGEON: I'll find him a field marshal if necessary. Just get him. (NURSE *turns away.*) And get the anaesthetist. (NURSE *turns away again.*) And get the last one changed.

NURSE: (*Turns back, clicks his heels.*) Yes, ma'am!

(*The* NURSE *goes out.* LENNY *is at the door.*)

Why don't you go home?

LENNY: I'm in more trouble there than I am here.

(*The* NURSE *leads him away as they talk, towards right.*)

. . . Anyway, I like it here – got any overnight facilities. . . ?

RITCHIE: . . . I still feel faint.

SURGEON: That will soon go away, I promise you.

RITCHIE: Are you sure, sister?

(*Pause. She looks at him.*)

SURGEON: I'm not a sister.

RITCHIE: Sorry, nurse.
SURGEON: I'm not a nurse.

(RITCHIE *looks up at her as she turns away to prepare. It dawns on him who she is. He puts his hands in his dressing gown pockets and slowly brings his gown further across himself. He crosses his legs and whines quietly.*)

THE PREPARATION ROOM

We see the NURSE *and the* ANAESTHETIST *walk across the corridor as Ritchie's scene finishes. They enter the Preparation Room.* MALCOLM *is on the edge of the bed.*

NURSE: Mr Thomas, please, if you would. Mrs Thomas?

(*The* NURSE *looks behind the door for her.*)

MALCOLM: Gone.

NURSE: Oh well, never mind, if you would care to lie down for our anaesthetist, Mr Thomas, while he has a little look at you . . .

(MALCOLM *lies on the trolley. The* NURSE *goes out and into the Waiting Room. The* ANAESTHETIST *checks* MALCOLM *over.*)

THE WAITING ROOM

GEORGE *is dozing.* JEAN *is glancing at a magazine. The* NURSE *pops his head around the door.*

NURSE: Mr Hill, I'll be asking you . . . *Mr Hill.*

GEORGE: (*Wakes with a start.*) That twat J. M. Barrie!

NURSE: What?

GEORGE: What?

NURSE: I'll be asking you to get changed soon, Mr Hill.

JEAN: I'll tell him.

(*The* NURSE *exits and returns to the Preparation Room.*)

The nurse said . . .

GEORGE: I heard him. I sometimes hear more than they think . . . Do people ever listen to me, Jean?

JEAN: They have little alternative.

GEORGE: Do they think I'm crazy?

JEAN: Does it matter?

GEORGE: Who to?

JEAN: You.

GEORGE: No, does it buggery! The thing is I need a public platform, that's what I need . . . do you think I *should* stand for Parliament?

JEAN: (*Quieter*) I wouldn't. Not if you still want people to listen to you.

GEORGE: What?

(JEAN *shakes her head.*)

THE PREPARATION ROOM

The ANAESTHETIST *has prepared the injection.*

ANAESTHETIST: . . . There we are, just relax now, Mr Thomas . . . and count down from ten for me, would you . . . (*He injects* MALCOLM.) . . . starting from now . . .

MALCOLM: Ten, nine, eight, seven . . . (*Starts getting drowsy but fights it.*) . . . six, five, four . . . three . . . two . . . one . . .

(*And gone.*)

NURSE: We have lift off.

ANAESTHETIST: I've never had anybody get down to one before.

NURSE: Perhaps counting backwards has some relevance to him.

(*They begin to take the trolley out.*)

THE WAITING ROOM

We see DOREEN *approaching the waiting room from stage right. She is struggling with a large suitcase. Enters the room.*

DOREEN: Excuse me, you don't . . .

GEORGE: No bugger told me to bring a suitcase. What do you want a suitcase for?

DOREEN: It's my husband's, it's . . .

GEORGE: What?

DOREEN: You know – emergency set of clothing, nothing to worry about. Just yet. Sorry to bother you, but you don't happen to have seen a naked man about thirty-five years old, do you? Lean body, rather attractive, flair for words?

JEAN: I should be so lucky.

GEORGE: What?

DOREEN: Possibly walking bow-legged and gritting his teeth?

JEAN: Afraid not.

DOREEN: Thank you.

JEAN: Think nothing of it, chuck.

(DOREEN *struggles towards the doors with the suitcase.*)

GEORGE: *What?*

JEAN: She was looking for a naked man.

GEORGE: Is she particular?

(*He laughs, and the laughter fades into snores.*)

THE CORRIDOR

The NURSE *and the* ANAESTHETIST *have given up the search for Malcolm's clothes and have brought the trolley into the corridor, stage left. We can see the trolley peeping out through the climbing plants and frames.*

NURSE: Mrs Thomas. Your husband thought you'd gone.

DOREEN: Wrong again. Is he unconscious?

NURSE: Yes.

DOREEN: Oh good. I like him best of all when he's unconscious.

(*She goes off, stage right, with suitcase.*)

THE WAITING ROOM

The NURSE *watches her go and then enters the Waiting Room.*

NURSE: Mr Hill, please.

(JEAN *gently wakes him up.*)

GEORGE: What!

NURSE: If you could take your husband next door, Mrs Hill, I'll be with you shortly.

(*He goes off stage right.* JEAN *helps* GEORGE *up. They move out of the room into the Preparation Room as they talk.*)

JEAN: Come on, George . . .
GEORGE: I'm tired. All that sodding talking.
JEAN: You shouldn't bother. People have to find out for themselves.
(*They exit, towards Preparation Room.*)
GEORGE: What?
JEAN: People. They have to find out for themselves.

THE PREPARATION ROOM
GEORGE *enters ahead of* JEAN.
GEORGE: Which is why most of the sodding world knows nothing.
(*We see the* NURSE *hustling back into the room with a dressing gown, and a basket.*)
NURSE: . . . If you would undress for me, Mr Hill, here's a dressing gown for you.
JEAN: I'll tell him.
NURSE: Mrs Hill, if you wish you can stay with your husband, or we can supply some light refreshment at Reception.
GEORGE: What?
JEAN: Do you want me to stay, George?
GEORGE: Ah, take my shoes off and then you can do what you want, girl.
JEAN: Let's have your jacket first.
(JEAN *takes his jacket off. The* NURSE *goes off stage right.* GEORGE *sits down to get his shoes taken off.*)
GEORGE: Don't lose my kidney donor card, Jean. (*She laughs.*) Hey no, if I can't live for ever, I want my vital organs to have a go.
JEAN: (*Quietly*) Whoever gets your eardrums'll have fun.
GEORGE: What?
JEAN: Nothing, love. Now are you sure you'll be all right?
GEORGE: Course I will. Piece of piss.
JEAN: Right, see you later.
(*She kisses the top of his head and walks to doorway. As she goes, she sees the* ANAESTHETIST *in the corridor with the*

trolley and MALCOLM.)

THE OPERATING THEATRE

The SURGEON *has been preparing herself, washing her hands, making case notes, preparing the instruments. She now turns towards* RITCHIE.

SURGEON: Now then, Mr . . . (*She just gets there before him.*) Burrows! Feeling better? Of course you are, a big strong man like you, why don't you sit up while I take your pulse and look into the whites of your eyes, although I'm sure there's absolutely nothing to worry about.

RITCHIE: It was the . . . that scream.

SURGEON: Of course it was. Have you known the man long?

RITCHIE: We went to school together.

SURGEON: It would appear he hasn't left the playground . . .

(*We hear the* NURSE *and* LENNY *outside.*)

NURSE: Get back in that room and stay there!

LENNY: Can't I watch?

(*The* NURSE *enters through the swing doors. He goes to approach the* SURGEON, *then glances around. Just in time to see* LENNY'*s face appear at the window to one of the doors. The* NURSE *goes back and opens the door.*)

Are you *sure* I can't watch?

(*The* NURSE *takes hold of him, moves him away.*)

NURSE: (*Off*) Now lie down . . .

(*The* SURGEON *is checking* RITCHIE'*s pulse. The* NURSE *returns, but waits at the doors.*)

SURGEON: (*Impatiently*) The patient's pulse is perfectly normal, I think we can begin now. Right, nurse?

(*He nods but stays where he is. The* SURGEON *turns away to bring the trolley into place. And we see* LENNY *again framed in the door window, peeping in. The* NURSE *pulls the door open wide. We see* LENNY *leaning against the door-frame with a charming yet manic smile on his face. The* NURSE *lets the door swing back as hard as he can, straight at* LENNY. *The* NURSE *then re-opens the door and we see* LENNY *about to move away, holding his nose gingerly.*)

(*Turning back*) If you would remove Mr Burrows' dressing gown, please.

(*The* NURSE *begins to take Ritchie's dressing gown off as the* SURGEON *prepares the hypodermic needle. We see that* RITCHIE *is still in his underpants. The* SURGEON *looks down at them. Looks at* RITCHIE. RITCHIE *looks down at them. Looks at the* SURGEON.)

You haven't taken your underpants off, Mr Burrows.

RITCHIE: Er no, I er wasn't sure . . . I mean, *before*, I er . . . should I take them off now?

SURGEON: (*Evenly*) Yes, I think so. Otherwise it would be somewhat similar to performing brain surgery on a man wearing a trilby hat.

RITCHIE: I'll . . . yes.

(*He gets off the operating table, smartly. The* SURGEON *sighs.*)

Shall I take them off out there?

SURGEON: If you don't want a vasectomy now, please tell me. Tell me *now*. You wouldn't be the first and you won't be the last, but I do have a lot still to do and time is running out.

RITCHIE: I er . . . the . . . when I fainted . . . I still feel . . . and well . . . I've had a bad time lately . . . the recession . . . it's er . . .

(SURGEON *coldly cuts him short and releases his arm.*)

SURGEON: Fine, as long as I know. Take Mr . . . (*Quietly*) Jeez . . .

NURSE: Burrows.

SURGEON: Take Mr Burrows out, please, nurse, and bring down the next patient.

(*The* NURSE *takes* RITCHIE *to the doors. As they get there, the doors open inward. It is* LENNY.)

LENNY: *Bottle gone, has it, Big Jobs?*

RITCHIE: I've changed my mind. (*Turns back.*) I'll go through with it. I want to have it now!

(RITCHIE *throws himself on the table. Lies down.*)

SURGEON: (*Wild*) YOU! Get out of here!

(LENNY *moves further into the room. He takes the brush from the* NURSE.)

LENNY: All right, Big Jobs. Let's be having you.

(NURSE *takes the brush from* LENNY.)

RITCHIE: Get off!

SURGEON: You two – get out! Go on, I said 'get out'!

RITCHIE: Who me?

SURGEON: Yes, both of you.

RITCHIE: What have I done?

LENNY: Yeah, what has he done?

SURGEON: Mr Gilbert, bring the next patient down.

RITCHIE: What about me?

(LENNY *as he talks puts his arm around* RITCHIE, *gently pushes him down on the operating table.* RITCHIE *is in such a state, he allows* LENNY *to do it at first.*)

LENNY: That's victimization, that is. You stay where you are.

SURGEON: Oh get off there and go away. What is this, have they let you two out for the day?

RITCHIE: I'd have been fine without him.

LENNY: It's true.

RITCHIE: So why won't you leave me alone, f'Christ's sake!

LENNY: (*Flat and hard*) For old times' sake, Big Jobs, for the days of sulphur, saltpetre and carbon.

RITCHIE: *What?*

LENNY: The components of a bomb.

RITCHIE: I knew it. I fucking knew it.

(RITCHIE *stands and charges at* LENNY, *knocking the* NURSE *aside.* LENNY *runs through the doors, swinging them outwards wildly as he runs. The doors swing backwards and hit* RITCHIE *as he runs out.*)

SURGEON: Well, don't just stand there – do something – bring the next patient down.

(*We hear the noise of battle from outside as the* NURSE *stares at her. He turns away and goes out of the doors.*)

THE CORRIDOR

As the NURSE *turns away from the* SURGEON *in the Operating Theatre, we see* LENNY *running across the corridor from right to left. Seconds later he is followed by* RITCHIE. *Then we see the* NURSE *walking across, from right to left. He gets as far as the Waiting Room doors.*

NURSE: Mr Martin, can we have the next . . .

(*At which point, the trolley and* MALCOLM *go hurtling towards him, from left to right along the corridor. He backs out of sight trying to stop the trolley. And we seee* LENNY *following after the trolley. We then see* RITCHIE *and the* ANAESTHETIST *coming from near the Preparation Room doorway, along the corridor.* LENNY *pushes the trolley wildly towards both men. He gets to the Waiting Room doors. Pushes the trolley past the door, into* RITCHIE *and the* ANAESTHETIST, *knocking them back.* LENNY *then turns the trolley and pulls it into the Waiting Room, through the doors.*)

THE WAITING ROOM

As LENNY *pulls the trolley with* MALCOLM *into the room, the* ANAESTHETIST *manages to get hold of the other end.* RITCHIE *is behind him.* LENNY *then pushes the trolley forcefully, knocking the* ANAESTHETIST *back into* RITCHIE, *who is knocked into the corridor briefly, where he is joined by the* NURSE, *who picks him up. The* ANAESTHETIST *is winded and bends double with the blow. He half crawls to a chair.* RITCHIE *re-enters, wildly. The* NURSE *is in the doorway, staring at them.* RITCHIE *gets hold of one end of the trolley.* LENNY *tries to push him into a corner and trap him. He also uses the trolley as a shield, spinning it on occasion.* MALCOLM *lies still and unknowing.* LENNY *and* RITCHIE *are 'talking' to each other as the opportunity arises.*

RITCHIE: I wish we were still at school, I'm telling you.

LENNY: But that's the trouble, isn't it, Big Jobs. You've grown up and no one's scared of you any more.

RITCHIE: At least I never tried to kill anyone. You tried to kill me!

(*He ends up shouting. And we hear* MALCOLM *suddenly speak, flat and cold.*)

MALCOLM: 'Attack Warning Red.'

(RITCHIE *tries to go below the trolley,* LENNY *goes above. They face each other across* MALCOLM. *The* ANAESTHETIST *tries to get hold of* RITCHIE *in passing. Gets knocked backwards. And the* NURSE *tries to grab* RITCHIE.)

NURSE: Stop it!

RITCHIE: Piss off!

(RITCHIE *knocks the* NURSE *away from him.*)

LENNY: The voice of reason – totally ignored. *But this is how the world will end, Big Jobs – with a pair of pillocks like you and me, who'll kill the fucking lot of us!*

(RITCHIE *lurches across the trolley, and* MALCOLM. RITCHIE *misses* LENNY, *but as he lands on* MALCOLM*'s stomach,* MALCOLM *rears up. Faces out, speaks and then falls back.*)

RITCHIE: (*As he lurches*) I'm warning you.

MALCOLM: (*As* RITCHIE *lands on him*) *'Repeat Attack Warning Red.'*

LENNY: Just like the TA – Russia's attacking and he's talking in his sleep.

(RITCHIE *makes another grab across the trolley. Gets hold of Lenny's dressing gown and pulls.* LENNY *jerks backwards and releases himself.* RITCHIE *lands on* MALCOLM *again.* MALCOLM *grabs hold of* RITCHIE*'s dressing gown, tries to pull him down. And we hear* MALCOLM *shout, suddenly and in terror.*)

MALCOLM: *Doreen!*

(RITCHIE *releases himself.* LENNY *looks down at* MALCOLM. *And* RITCHIE *leaps again for* LENNY, *gets hold of him properly by his dressing gown, and hauls* LENNY, *spreadeagled, over the trolley and* MALCOLM. RITCHIE *pushes/throws* LENNY *away from him, downstage. He goes to follow him. The* NURSE *gets hold of* RITCHIE, *tightly by both arms, pulls him away from*

LENNY, *like a father with a child in tantrum.* RITCHIE *begins to scream.*)

THE PREPARATION ROOM

As RITCHIE *breaks down and screams,* GEORGE *rears up in bed.*

GEORGE: *What!*

(*. . . and lies down again immediately.*)

THE OPERATING THEATRE

As RITCHIE *screams, the* SURGEON *curses, and goes storming out of the doors of the Operating Theatre.*

THE WAITING ROOM

We see RITCHIE *and* LENNY, *both on the floor, downstage, facing each other across the room.*

RITCHIE: I didn't know what I was doing, then at school, I was a kid, *a big kid, that's all – and nobody stopped me.* Nobody stopped me once. They all let me do it.

(*The* SURGEON *enters as he talks. Looks around, laughs.*)

I want to murder you, you bastard . . . but I can't . . .

SURGEON: Oh the pleasures of the *hoi polloi.*

(RITCHIE *is huddled up like a scared child.*)

RITCHIE: I can't do anything . . . any more . . . (*He breaks down.* LENNY *approaches.*)

LENNY: So this is revenge. . . . 'An eye for an eye turns the whole world blind.' Mahatma Gandhi, Big Jobs.

(*The* SURGEON *turns to go back. Talks as she goes. She reaches the door and looks down the corridor, stage right.*)

SURGEON: . . . There are times when I do so regret the Peasants' Revolt . . .

(*The* SURGEON *begins to back away into the room, stunned.*)

What in God's name . . . Right that is it. You have two minutes to leave, the lot of you. When I come back I wish to find you gone. Mr Gilbert, Mr Martin . . .

(SURGEON *and* ANAESTHETIST *exeunt.*)

DOREEN: (*Off and faintly*) Lenny . . .

(*We see* DOREEN *enter the corridor.* DOREEN *is wearing an army-issue nuclear survival suit. The one-piece outer garment is made of PVC, backed into knitted nylon. It comes complete with hood. (For our purposes the inner suit of lightweight charcoal-coloured cloth is not needed.) She is also wearing a black rubber face-respirator with a polycarbonate visor and a NATO respirator cartridge, heavy-duty gauntlets and steel-braced wellingtons. Her magnificent gesture/grand entrance is spoilt somewhat when she walks straight into the door-frame. She speaks dully from behind the respirator.*)

Lenny . . . it's me, Lenny!

LENNY: Well I'm not going to Llangollen with you dressed like that.

(*She takes the respirator off.*)

DOREEN: But this is it, Lenny; my husband's special-issue suit. I pinched it from his suitcase.

NURSE: Oh, Mrs Thomas, please . . .

DOREEN: Stay away! I haven't even started yet. This is just the hors d'oeuvres.

(DOREEN *leans over* MALCOLM *talking urgently and close to him.*)

'Attack Warning Red, repeat Attack Warning Red.'

NURSE: Mrs Thomas . . .

DOREEN: Shut up! Malcolm, 'Attack Warning Red' *Malcolm!* 'Atta—.'

(MALCOLM *starts his learnt litany, toneless at first.*)

MALCOLM: 'Attack Warning Red. Repeat. Attack Warning Red. Government procedure is as follows: There will be no public warning of nuclear attack. Repeat no public warning.'

RITCHIE: I didn't know what I was doing . . .

MALCOLM: 'All civilian attempts at escape to be stopped. Citizens to stay indoors on penalty of death . . .' (*He sits forward in panic, hands reaching out.*)

Oh, Doreen . . .

DOREEN: Now do you see, Lenny?
LENNY: Of course I do; that's the trouble.

(DOREEN *pushes up the part of the trolley where the head and shoulders of the patient rest, so that when* MALCOLM *falls back he is in a semi-vertical position.*)

DOREEN: 'Contingency plans.'
NURSE: Mrs Thomas!
DOREEN: 'Contingency plans.'
NURSE: Stop her.
DOREEN: '*Contingency plans.*'
MALCOLM: 'Contingency plans for Government survival come into operation immediately. The chief executive of the county council will become controller for this area. I am the chief executive of the county council.'
RITCHIE: I was a big kid, that's all, a big kid – and nobody stopped me.
MALCOLM: 'I will go down to the protected bunker.'
GEORGE: . . . An awfully big adventure! Silly twat!
MALCOLM: (*Panic begins again.*) 'I will leave my . . . I will leave my . . . my . . .' no . . . NO!
DOREEN: 'I will leave my family . . . *I WILL LEAVE MY FAMILY!*'

(MALCOLM *fights against saying it.*)

MALCOLM: 'I will . . . I . . .' No. No!

(DOREEN *looks at* LENNY *who starts laughing.*)

LENNY: It's quite simple really. Those who don't count . . . don't live.

(*He continues laughing.*)

NURSE: What's funny about that?
LENNY: Nothing. Still, you've got to look on the bright side. At least it'll get rid of mass unemployment.

(*Laughs again.*)

MALCOLM: (*Rambling in parts.*) 'Lay magistrates and chief executives of the County Council will have absolute power of life and death . . . They are . . .'

(*The* NURSE *rushes at the trolley. Slams the headrest down so that* MALCOLM *bounces into a horizontal position.*)

MALCOLM: '. . . They are empowered to hold special . . . courts . . .' Doreen!

DOREEN: (*To* LENNY) But there must be something we can do. There must.

LENNY: Yes. At the onset of a nuclear attack, you can bend with your head between your legs, and kiss your arse goodbye.

DOREEN: LENNY!

MALCOLM: Doreen . . .

(SURGEON *enters with* ANAESTHETIST.)

SURGEON: Mrs Thomas – this clinic is no longer prepared to take any responsibility for you, your husband, or your associates. Your husband will very shortly regain consciousness and I would ask you to remove yourselves as soon as he does so. Mr Martin, if you would attend to Mr . . . Mr . . .

NURSE: (*Automatically*) Burrows.

SURGEON: Mr Burrows. The next patient please, Mr Gilbert.

NURSE: *Right.*

(*The* NURSE *goes to the Preparation Room. The* SURGEON *goes to the Operating Theatre.*)

MALCOLM: 'The Prime Minister will be conducting the war from either a secret bunker or an aircraft circling Northern Ireland. He or she . . .'

(LENNY *puts his hand over* MALCOLM*'s mouth, firmly.*)

LENNY: You see, nobody in their right mind would think of bombing Northern Ireland . . . except the . . . Irish themselves.

(*In the Preparation Room* GEORGE *is fast asleep.*)

NURSE: Mr Hill . . . Mr Hill. . . !

GEORGE: What? You said you had a headache! What? (*And asleep.*)

ANAESTHETIST: Mr Burrows . . .

RITCHIE: You know when you grow up . . . no really, when you grow up.

ANAESTHETIST: Yes, come and lie down, Mr Burrows . . . really, a nice rest.

(*The* ANAESTHETIST *leads* RITCHIE *to the Preparation Room. The* NURSE *crosses towards the Operating Theatre.*)

DOREEN: Lenny, there is something we can do!

LENNY: Oh yes? Retaliate first?

DOREEN: Right. At the onset of war before they retire underground to press their precious buttons on our behalf . . .

LENNY: Thank you very much.

DOREEN: . . . we assassinate them.

LENNY: Only trouble is, Doreen, it's er . . . murder. You can't honestly be equivocal about that, mmmmm?

(RITCHIE *and the* ANAESTHETIST *enter the Preparation Room.*)

RITCHIE: Well here we are then. Having a . . .

ANAESTHETIST: Yes. Just lie down Mr . . . (*Sees* GEORGE *on bed.*) Oh.

DOREEN: How about self-defence?

ANAESTHETIST: Just sit down, Mr Burrows.

LENNY: No. Murder.

RITCHIE: (*Sitting down*) Call me Big Jobs.

DOREEN: But we have to start somewhere.

LENNY: Yes. So where do you want to start? (*Indicates* MALCOLM.) Here? (*They both look down on him.*) This is your man.

(NURSE *enters Operating Theatre.*)

SURGEON: Well?

NURSE: I don't think you're going to like this. But the next vasectomy patient is seventy-seven years old, almost fully clothed and fast asleep.

SURGEON: Jesus Chr— (*Phone rings.*) Yes?

LENNY: Because that's what it means, Doreen. It means we become just like them – just like the people we despise. In the end I think I'd rather die first.

RITCHIE: Do you remember when it was really nice?

SURGEON: No, I don't.

LENNY: Do you . . . you know, love him?

RITCHIE: You know, growing up, in the fifties.

SURGEON: I realize that.
DOREEN: I dunno. I used to.
ANAESTHETIST: I was hardly born then. Big Jobs.
SURGEON: Wonderful.
MALCOLM: Doreen.
RITCHIE: Remember when . . .
MALCOLM: Given some kind of advanced warning . . .
RITCHIE: Pendletons Twicers . . .
MALCOLM: . . . deaths . . .
RITCHIE: . . . were tuppence?
GEORGE: What?
RITCHIE: Pendletons.
MALCOLM: . . . can be reduced to possibly twenty million.
GEORGE: Pendleton? There was a widow in Southport called Pendleton.
SURGEON: I know all that.
GEORGE: By Christ, now there was a woman! She were a twicer all right.
MALCOLM: Oh you don't know, you don't know.
ANAESTHETIST: Oh, Mr Hill, please.
SURGEON: Yes, yes.
LENNY: Listen, I think I should go now.
SURGEON: Yes we have a patient, but we have no nurse. (*She looks at the* NURSE. *He holds the look.*)
DOREEN: Lenny.
SURGEON: John. . . ?
NURSE: No.
DOREEN: *Lenny.*
SURGEON: So? So you send the girl home, she has her baby – who knows, it might live long enough to thank us.
(*She slams the phone down. Glares at the* NURSE. *He goes towards the Preparation Room.*)
But I doubt it.
DOREEN: I think you're wonderful, Lenny.
LENNY: Call me Clint and I'll . . .
DOREEN: Give me a quick Llangollen?
LENNY: Or even a slow Ffestiniog.

(*They both shake their heads.*)
But I'll see you again? (*She nods.*) We'll carry banners together. We'll march for peace. It's better than nothing and much better than Blackpool. (*He looks towards the phone.*) But first of all, there's a couple of things I've got to do.

MALCOLM: (*Appearing to regain consciousness*) Oh . . . Doreen . . . I'm so scared, Doreen . . . I'm, . . . I . . .

LENNY: (*Feeling for non-existent pockets*) Can you lend me 10p?

(*The* NURSE *has crossed and entered the Preparation Room. Sees* RITCHIE *on the chair and* GEORGE *on the bed.*)

DOREEN: I . . . yes, in my bag . . .

(LENNY *is already half-way to her bag before she speaks. He goes to the phone and begins to dial.*)

MALCOLM: . . . I'm not scared for me . . .

NURSE: How are you doing?

ANAESTHETIST: Not getting much sense out of these two.

RITCHIE: Take my advice, it's not nice when you grow up.

GEORGE: Don't be bloody daft, lad, where there's life there's hope!

(*The* NURSE *returns to the Operating Theatre.*) (DOREEN *hugs* MALCOLM *and holds him as he sits up bewildered.*)

LENNY: Hello, Monica? Yes . . . yes . . . no, no I haven't. Not yet. No, I want to talk to you. No no, I don't want to talk about that, that's no problem any more. Listen . . . *LISTEN*. When I come home, I want to sit down with you, and I want to talk to you about Nicaragua.

(*He throws the phone down. Perhaps ruffles* DOREEN'*s hair as he exits towards the Operating Theatre.*)

NURSE: (*As* LENNY *enters the Operating Theatre*) Look, I think we're finished for today, the old man doesn't seem to know whether it's now or Christmas, I'm going to . . .

(LENNY *bursts through the doors, his dressing gown is off.*)

LENNY: All right, all right. I kid you not. This time.

(*Gets on table. Still and silent as they look at him. Then he screams long and real.*)
AAAAAAAAAAAAAGGGGGGGGGGGHHHHH-HHHHHHHH!
(*Lights out.*)

IT'S A MADHOUSE

CHARACTERS

PETE	*Patient, mid thirties*
EDDIE	*Male nurse, late fifties*
MARIE	*Patient, late thirties*
CHRISTINE	*Auxiliary nurse, early forties*
BEN	*Patient, late sixties*
VERA	*Patient, early twenties*
JIMMY	*Husband, early forties*

The action takes place in the psychiatric ward of a general hospital in the north-west of England.

It's a Madhouse was first presented at the Contact Theatre, Manchester, in May and June 1976. The cast was as follows:

EDDIE	Kenneth Alan Taylor
JIMMY	Oz Clark
PETE	David Mallinson
CHRISTINE	Patricia Hennigan
MARIE	Sally Gibson
BEN	Sam Kelly
VERA	Jean Warren
Director	Caroline Smith
Designer	Marty Flood

Dark. Quiet.

A song is murmured in the padded cell, stage right. 'Rock-a-Bye Baby'. *The rhythm becomes more intense, faster.* WOMAN'*s voice. We soon become aware that she is walking around the cell, hitting the wall and the door in rhythm to the song. Brings it to a crescendo. Like a boil bursting. Silence.*

Then a phone rings loudly. It is amplified.

The lights come up on the set, revealing PETE *stage left sitting in his chair, dressed straight off Waikiki, painting, then looking at a travel brochure. The phone is still ringing.*

PETE: (*Reading from the brochure*) To see all that Hawaii has to offer would take a lifetime . . .

(EDDIE, *the male nurse, hurries in. Goes to the phone. Just as he gets there, it stops. He turns away, takes his own coat off. Puts a white coat on. Looks briefly at the reports left on his desk by the staff of the previous shift. We hear a sobbing noise from the padded cell.* EDDIE *looks briefly through the peephole, then glances over at* PETE *as* PETE *continues to read aloud.*)

Hawaii is a land of waterfalls, orchids an' volcanic peaks . . . the most romantic setting in the world . . .

(EDDIE *moves towards* PETE, *stands watching him, looking over his shoulder.*)

. . . Here it is, Eddie, here it is, look – 'A Holiday Of A Lifetime'!

EDDIE: Two weeks in Sunny Runcorn?

PETE: Visit the Polynesian Cultural Centre, see authentic communities still in existence, where every September Hawaii's most extravagant entertainment is staged. 'Invitation to Paradise'. (*Puts the brochure down, counts on his fingers.*) May, June, July, August, September. Easy. Dead easy.

(MARIE *sobs suddenly from the cell.* EDDIE *goes across to the cell as he talks.* PETE *is immediately anxious in case he goes away.*)

EDDIE: D'y'think so? An' where are y'goin' t'get the money?

PETE: Hitch-hike, Eddie, hitch-hike.

EDDIE: (*Looks through the peephole, then turns back to* PETE.) Oh aye, there's always lots of lorries goin' t' Hawaii. Straight off the M62, down the M57 to the docks, turn left at the Isle of Man. What're you goin' t'do then? Walk on water? (*Starts to come back.*) Don't tell me we'll have t'put you on the Jesus Ward. (*Smiles.*) You'd like the Jesus Ward, Pete, two dozen Jesus Christs, all fightin' like hell. (*Mimics*) 'I'm Jesus.' 'No y'not, I am.' 'Y'not see, cos it's me, my dad said so an' he should know!'

PETE: I'm goin' t'work me passage, so there.

EDDIE: Work y'passage? You? Y'won't reach Holyhead in that case, never mind Hawaii. Y'the only person I know needs three seasick pills before he gets in the bath.

PETE: We'll see about that. My dad were a sailor, you know – don't get many sailors in Sheffield, 'cept on the boatin' lake of a Sunday afternoon. Went everywhere my dad did. Sailed the seven seas. (*Pause.*) An' never found his way back t'Sheffield.

EDDIE: (*Quickly*) So anyroad, young Peter, when y' thinkin' of goin'?

PETE: T'night.

EDDIE: That soon? I'd better get the kitchens t'send over some sandwiches. An' a packet of Marzine.

PETE: A flask of tea'd come in handy. An' a map of the world.

(EDDIE *turns away towards the exit by the padded cell.* PETE *picks up his paint brush. Stops. Shouts out, as he does on nearly every occasion that* EDDIE *leaves him.*)

Barry! Barry!

EDDIE: (*Turns. Adopts a deeper voice. A voice he will keep for all the* 'BARRY' *scenes.*) Yes, Peter?

PETE: Barry . . .

EDDIE: What is it, me old China?

PETE: Y'll stop them gettin' me, won't yer? Y'll make sure

I'm not . . .

EDDIE: I'll stop them, don't worry . . .

PETE: 'Cos y'know, I'm goin', honest to God I'm goin', I shouldn't have come here to college in the first place. It was too much for me, and I can't keep hiding in your room any more. They're going to find me. But I'm going t'night, don't worry, back t'Sheffield. Across the moors in the dead of night. Like Attila The Hun.

EDDIE: Oh . . . well, er I'd better cancel the seasick pills.

PETE: There's no sea between here an' Sheffield, Barry.

EDDIE: Of course not, got muddled there for a bit, y'know . . . never was any good at geography.

(EDDIE *goes out, after taking one last look at* MARIE *through the peephole.* PETE *moves towards the goldfish bowl.*)

PETE: You an' me, hey Jaws? What d'y'say? On the road together. Need some company when I'm out there on my own . . .

(*As he speaks,* CHRISTINE *enters through the opposite exit to the one* EDDIE *went out of. Two suitcases in her hands. Black eye. Stands behind* PETE *as he talks.*)

. . . facin' the elements side by side, like . . . like . . . the Ancient Mariner (*Sees* CHRISTINE.) . . . an' . . .

(*Turns and scuttles back to his painting. Will not look at her.*)

CHRISTINE: Hello, Peter.

(*He mumbles, head down.*)

Don't get upset, better than talkin' to yourself. I often chat to our canary. (*She is walking towards the nurses' room as she talks. Puts her suitcases down in a corner, comes back.*) Miserable old sod it is and all. Doesn't even chirp.

PETE: (*With conviction*) Jaws knows me, y'know. He bloody well does. Sees my face up against the glass an' he goes racing around the bowl.

CHRISTINE: I know he does, I've seen it myself.

(BEN *comes crashing through the swing doors that* CHRISTINE *has just come through. He is riding a delivery bike. A box of groceries still in the metal frame between the handlebars. He stands the bike up in a corner. Looks around. Sees* CHRISTINE, *pauses, takes a slip of paper off the top of the groceries.*)

BEN: Mrs Pugh? 5 Belmont Road?

(CHRISTINE *just stares at him.* BEN *lifts the grocery box up and totters over to her. Stands in front of her.*)

Where do y'want them, missus? (*Pause.*) Hey? (*He waits. No answer. Drops the box at her feet.*) Fuck you then. Woman.

CHRISTINE: Been out shoppin', Ben?

BEN: Fuck off. I don't talk to strange women.

PETE: Got any ciggies in there?

BEN: No, I already looked. (*Holds up a plastic bag with a pair of kippers in it.*) Got some kippers though, they're a good smoke. (*Shakes with laughter.*)

(EDDIE *re-enters. Does not see the bike in the corner.* BEN *refuses to look at* EDDIE, *who stands right in front of him.*)

EDDIE: Where the bloody hell did y'get them?

BEN: The Co-op. They give you stamps as well.

EDDIE: (*Snatches the kippers. Glances at his watch.*) Since when have you done your Occupational Therapy on the kipper counter in the Co-op?

BEN: He had us makin' table tennis bats again, an' I stuck the pimples the wrong way round an' he shouted at me, an' anyway I don't even like table tennis. (*Takes a quick look at* EDDIE*'s face. Looks down again.*) So I went for a walk an' got a job at the Co-op.

EDDIE: Is that a fact. Well I never, fancy that.

BEN: It's a nice job, they give yer a bike.

(EDDIE *looks again at the box on the floor, looks at* BEN, *turns around, sees the bike.*)

EDDIE: Oh God no.

BEN: The front tyre's a bit flat or somethin'. Someone must have stole the pump. Maybe I could make one in Therapy.

EDDIE: D'you know what you have done, Ben? Do y'? Can y' work it out? Just look at the box, look at the bike an' then have a good look around y'self. Go on.

(BEN *does as he is told. Then looks at* EDDIE.)

BEN: Delivered them t'the wrong address?

EDDIE: (*Pushes* BEN *and laughs out loud.*) Y'stupid old sod.

CHRISTINE: Which Co-op?

BEN: I'm not speakin' to you.

EDDIE: Come on, Ben, which one?

BEN: I didn't go the shops. I didn't. It was outside a house as a matter of fact. On its own.

EDDIE: Oh, I see, someone must have lost it.

BEN: That's what I thought an' all.

EDDIE: So you took pity on the poor lonely kippers an' the miserable mayonnaise, the bacon breakin' its heart cryin' . . .

BEN: No, I'm not soft, I just wanted t'have a ride on a bike. Y'don't see many delivery bikes these days, tha' knows. (*Nods his head.*) The lad ran after me f'two blocks.

EDDIE: I'm sick of you, d'you know that? What am I goin' to say to the Co-op? Answer me that.

BEN: Ask them if they'll give a reward f'me capture and I'll go halves with y'.

(*We hear* MARIE *knocking quietly from the padded cell.* CHRISTINE *looks at* EDDIE *a he jokingly goes to cuff* BEN.)

EDDIE: It's Marie. Seems she drove the last shift up the wall. They ended up telling her the ambulance was here from the sub-normality hospital to take her back where she came from. And, of course, that made her ten times worse, and they had to put her in there.

CHRISTINE: Bring her out.

EDDIE: I'll do it now, you take your coat off. (*Turns back to* BEN.) An' you, put the box back on the bike, go on.

(EDDIE *goes over to the padded cell.* BEN *looks at the box, attempts to lift it, gives up, sits down.* CHRISTINE *goes over to the nurses' room, takes her coat off, drapes it over her suitcases so they cannot be seen.* EDDIE *opens the cell door.* MARIE *is there waiting. She has a ribbon in her hair but is otherwise dressed normally, although second-hand. She has hold of a teddy bear, trails it behind her as* EDDIE *walks her over to an easy chair.*)

Better now, chuck?

MARIE: Eh what . . . what?

EDDIE: Feelin' better?

MARIE: Teddy wee-weed on the floor.

EDDIE: I know, I saw.

MARIE: (*Quickly*) But Teddy never poo-pooed.

EDDIE: Teddy constipated.

MARIE: Naughty Tedd. (*Smacks it.*) I'm going to tell on you.

EDDIE: Who are y'going to tell?

MARIE: I'll tell a policeman. I'll phone them up.

EDDIE: Bugger for the phone, you are an' all. (*Sits her down.*) Get you into trouble one of these days, it will that. Ambulances to the cemetery, fire brigade to the swimmin' baths, I don't know . . .

MARIE: More fools them f'going, that's what I say.

EDDIE: Y'll not learn will you, not till it's too late.

MARIE: An' what'll they do to me, Eddie? Take me away again? Lock me up? (*Laughs.*) With Wee Willie Winkie and the ghosties. Me and Teddy . . .

EDDIE: (*Not said harshly*) . . . pissing past y'selves, the pair of you . . .

(*The phone rings* loudly *in the nurses' room.* CHRISTINE *jumps. She seems tempted to let it ring but the noise defeats her. Picks it up.*)

CHRISTINE: Churchill Ward . . . oh right. Eddie, it's for you. Admissions.

EDDIE: You're joking?

(*Comes across, picks up the phone.* MARIE *sits still, staring at her teddy hanging loosely from her hands.*)

At this time, surely not? (*Picks up the phone.*) Eddie here . . . not much notice, is it . . . man, woman or beast? . . . All right, I'll come down now. (*Puts the phone down.*) New patient *now*. At this time of the day, and not an emergency. But the admission ward's full. Again.

CHRISTINE: If his name's Jimmy and he's got 'Mother'

tattooed on his arm, say we don't want him.

EDDIE: (*At the doorway*) No, it's a woman. (*Looks at her.*) Been at you again, has he?

CHRISTINE: No more than normal.

EDDIE: Walk into a lamp-post then did you?

CHRISTINE: Back kitchen door actually.

EDDIE: Aye I know, one with legs. What was it this time? The peas not mushy enough?

CHRISTINE: (*Harsh laugh*) Not a bad guess. I ruined his tripe. I left it on the table an' when he got back from the British Legion, the cat was sat on it.

EDDIE: I don't know what you saw in him in the first place.

CHRISTINE: Well, you know what it's like, Eddie – you fall in love with a prince and when you marry him he turns into a frog.

EDDIE: (*As he goes*) You, you're a fool to yourself. You are. How many times have I told you? You want t'clear out while y'can. (*He walks away.*)

CHRISTINE: I know.

EDDIE: (*As he goes past* BEN) I want that box in there ready t'go when I get back, Ben, d'you hear me?

(BEN *appears to take no notice.* EDDIE *goes to the far doorway.*)

PETE: Barry, Barry! Where are y'goin', Barry?

EDDIE: Out of my mind, son.

PETE: Can I come?

(EDDIE *goes.* MARIE *looks up, watches* PETE.)

MARIE: Give us a ciggie.

(*No answer.*)

Petie, Petie, give us a ciggie. Go on.

PETE: Little girls aren't supposed t'smoke.

MARIE: Ah, go on, please.

PETE: Y'lungs'll drop off.

MARIE: Your willy'll drop off if I get hold of you. Give us a ciggie!

PETE: I haven't got any.

MARIE: Liar, liar, catch on fire. (*Pause.*) Give us a ciggie!

PETE: I haven't . . .

MARIE: I'll tell Eddie on you, I will, I'll tell him what you tried t'do t'me . . .

PETE: I didn't . . .

MARIE: Yes you did . . . doctors and nurses . . . submarines.

PETE: You wanted to . . .

MARIE: On Southport sands . . .

PETE: It was your idea . . .

MARIE: I'll still tell, I will, I will, I will . . .

PETE: I've only got the one.

MARIE: I only want one.

PETE: I was savin' it for tonight. On the road.

MARIE: What road?

PETE: Lots of them. The er M62 . . . the East Lancs . . .

MARIE: You're puddled.

PETE: No I'm not. I know the way. I worked it out in Occupational Therapy.

MARIE: (*The cigarette momentarily forgotten*) D'you know what – they had me makin' flower arrangements this afternoon. Till I bit the heads off three daffodils an' a tulip. The bloody tulip was plastic. An' me top set fell out. (*Pause.*) Go on, Petie, I'll give it back, promise.

PETE: I need it more than you.

MARIE: Give us that ciggie. (*She stands, advances slowly.*)

PETE: I . . . don't . . . want to.

MARIE: I'll use me hat pin on you.

PETE: Y'wouldn't.

MARIE: An' I'll kill y'goldfish!

PETE: You kill Jaws an' I'll . . . I'll . . . I'll . . .

(MARIE *grabs his drawing paper away from him and rips it into pieces. She drops the pieces around him.*)

MARIE: Now give us that ciggie . . . give us that ciggie . . .

(PETE *backs away from her, dropping his paint brush, knocking over his paper cup full of water.*)

PETE: (*Looking at his flip-flops*) That's not fair, I'm wet . . . I'm wet . . .

MARIE: Petie's wet himself . . . (*Loudly*) Petie's wet himself!

(CHRISTINE, *who has been reading the notes on her table, hears* MARIE *and comes out into the lounge.*)

CHRISTINE: All right, all right, what's going on?

MARIE: It wasn't me, it wasn't me, it was him, he's wet himself.

PETE: I never did, it was her, she ripped my paper.

MARIE: He pulled Teddy's fur.

PETE: An' she said dirty things.

MARIE: He got his little willy out!

PETE: I never, I never – an' it isn't little.

MARIE: 'Tis so . . .

CHRISTINE: Have you two quite finished?

MARIE: It's all his . . .

CHRISTINE: Do I have to remind you, Marie . . .

MARIE: (*To* PETE) You're dirty, you are, dirty, and I'm going to tell a police –

CHRISTINE: Remember where you come from, young lady, remember what's been said before by the day staff, remember the other hospital, remember how pleased you were to come here? Hey? Much nicer here, isn't it? All the amenities, the therapy?

MARIE: I don't like making flowers.

CHRISTINE: But you wouldn't like to go back there, would you? Mmmm, Marie love?

MARIE: I don't like you any more.

PETE: I'm not scared. You can't frighten . . .

(CHRISTINE *looks at him.*)

Er, I want another piece of paper. Please. And some more water.

(CHRISTINE *goes back into the nurses' room, opens a cupboard, takes out a white sheet of paper.*)

MARIE: (*Whispers*) You've had it, you have, I'm goin' to get my gang on to you tomorrow, me an' Babs an' the others . . . you an' your goldfish're dead men!

PETE: We won't be here tomorrow.

CHRISTINE: Here you are, Peter.

(*He takes the paper.* CHRISTINE *turns away.* MARIE *makes a half-hearted attempt to snatch at the paper.* PETE *cries out.* CHRISTINE *turns around, points at* MARIE *who puts her head down and sulks gloriously. She returns to her chair.* CHRISTINE *walks away.* PETE *realizes he has no water.*)

PETE: Nurse, nurse.

(*He holds up the empty cup.* CHRISTINE *has gone through the doors past the nurses' room.* MARIE *giggles.* PETE *takes a pace towards the doors, turns back, looks at* MARIE, *returns, takes his paper quickly. Walks away, comes back, grabs his paint brush, walks away again, comes back and takes his board. Goes off.*)

MARIE: (*As* BEN *stands and goes over the groceries*) Give us a ciggie, Ben. Go on.

BEN: They aren't on y'order, I looked. (*Finds the kippers again, realizes he hasn't said it to* MARIE.) Got these though. Kippers. They're a good smoke.

MARIE: I know where y'keep y'ciggies – in y'shoe. I know where they are.

BEN: Stayin' there too.

MARIE: Give us one.

BEN: Give y'somethin' else in a minute, woman, if you don't shut up.

(BEN *starts taking all the foodstuffs out of the box, puts the box back on the bike and slowly begins filling the box, first investigating the contents of each bag.*)

MARIE: I'm going to tell on you.

BEN: I don't care, it's a lousy bike. It wobbles.

MARIE: (*Looking at the food*) Got anythin' to poison goldfish? (*She looks, finds a packet of pepper, opens the lid, goes over to the goldfish bowl, shakes the packet massively over the tank.*)

BEN: Y'shouldn't put pepper on fish. Salt an' vinegar's much better.

(*They both giggle. The doors by the nurses' room open.* MARIE *puts the pepper pot at the side of the tank as* PETE *and* CHRISTINE *come through the doors. Both* BEN *and* MARIE *sidle suspiciously back to their seats.* CHRISTINE *has got hold of* PETE*'s arm lightly. She is carrying the water. He has the board and the paper, plus the paint brush behind his ear.*)

CHRISTINE: . . . How many times have I told you? Hey?

PETE: Dunno. Is Barry back yet?

CHRISTINE: He's down at reception, Peter, now listen to me for a change; you do not go into the women's toilets if you want water, or to pay a penny.

PETE: Men's is further away. Y'have t'go nearly outside t'go the men's.

CHRISTINE: And you do not wait around for someone to use them first.

PETE: I get frightened on me own.

CHRISTINE: Well, be warned, some of the girls might think it's funny, but Miss Urquhart is nearly eighty and thinks men carry it under their arms and it comes out of a tap. (CHRISTINE *ruffles his hair,* PETE *sits down, she puts the water down.* BEN *is reading the labels on every bottle and packet.* PETE *quietly feels under his arm.* CHRISTINE *walks over to* BEN. *He moves immediately away from her, skirts her like a dog with an intruder.*)

Let me give you a hand with them.

BEN: Stay away from them, woman.

CHRISTINE: Come on, you'll be all day, the butter'll melt.

BEN: Go on, keep away, I don't want your help.

CHRISTINE: (*Looks into the box on the bike.*) You haven't re-packed them very well, have you? Are those eggs on the bottom there?

BEN: Keep away from me . . . don't touch my box . . . I know your kind, I've seen how you operate, all sweetness and shite, I can tell, helpin' hands helpin' y'selves, the same as the others; suck a man dry, take my house an' home, everythin' I've got, lock me up here with these boobies an' babies, suicides, snot pickers, sex maniacs, ciggie robbers, I charge for listenin' you know, lady. Lady! Daughters, daughters, mothers, girls, wives, *women*!

CHRISTINE: I thought we might arrive back at women, somehow.

BEN: (*As he now furiously repacks the box*) As I arrived here, driven to it, in a car, down the years, over the edge, around the bend; at every corner, at every point, prick, prod, position – a woman, draining y' juices, diggin' y'grave. (*Mounts the bike, kicks the support away.*) I buried my wife last week. I'll just go and see if she's dead yet. (*He laughs wildly. Rides the bike towards the door he came in.* EDDIE *and* VERA *enter just as he gets there. He rides straight past them, through the open doors.*)

EDDIE: Ben . . . Ben!

(*We see him go. Miss a beat. Then the bike crashes.* BEN *cries out.* CHRISTINE *goes through the doorway to him.* EDDIE *goes to follow her but* VERA *walks towards centre where* MARIE *is already sitting up, noticing* VERA*'s obvious pregnancy.* EDDIE *goes across.* VERA *is carrying a cheap suitcase and she is clearly very young. She stares at* MARIE *as* MARIE *stares at her stomach.*)

I must order those no-cycling signs . . . Right, er Vera . . . (*Takes hold of her suitcases.*) You'll soon sort yourself out . . . it's not always as er . . . well, we do have our quiet moments you'll be relieved to learn . . . if you'll come with me, I'll show you where you can put your clothes . . .

(MARIE *and* VERA *still staring.* MARIE *slowly puts her hand out and touches* VERA*'s stomach.* VERA *recoils.*)

MARIE: Baybee . . . baybee . . . heheh, baybee . . .

EDDIE: What an observant little girl you are, Marie . . . (*Takes hold of* VERA.) . . . Right, Vera, let's get a move on, shall we? Tea-time soon, have a little chat then, get you organized . . . (*He looks closely at her.*) Haven't I seen you before somewhere?

VERA: No.

EDDIE: Funny . . . still, how have you arrived with us?

VERA: I'm informal.

EDDIE: Ah, you know that much, at least.

VERA: I went t'see my doctor, I told him I couldn't take no more, an' I had t'get away . . . everything was gettin' on top of me . . .

EDDIE: (*Recognizes her*) It was y'sister, wasn't it?

VERA: What sister?

EDDIE: Y'the dead spit. Like twins. Joan her name was . . . last year. Joan . . . what was her second name.

VERA: Wareham.

EDDIE: That's right. I remember. (*With no affection*) Very well.

VERA: Are you Eddie?

EDDIE: Indeed I am.

VERA: She remembers you an' all. I want a transfer to another ward.

EDDIE: A transfer? What d'you think you are – a footballer?

VERA: She was all right here till she met you.

EDDIE: Y'mean no one had spotted her till then?

VERA: She was sick.

EDDIE: Aye, an' I wish they were all as sick as her in here. Fred Pontin'd snap this place up straight away.

VERA: I'm not stayin' here.

EDDIE: Don't let me stop you.

VERA: You can't treat me like that, I'm not well, I've been told, my doctor said so.

EDDIE: Just like a doctor. Anything to empty the waiting room and go home.

VERA: He said I was on the edge of a nervous breakdown.

EDDIE: Oh, I see – so he sent you to a mental hospital so you could have one good and proper. Make a decent job of it.

VERA: I want to see a doctor.

(EDDIE *quietly offers her the suitcase back.*)

EDDIE: You've seen one already at reception and he sent you to me.

VERA: I want to see another one here now. That's what I've come for, treatment and help. So I can get better.

EDDIE: Y'might see a doctor on Monday. If y'lucky. Until then, you've got me.

VERA: I'm goin' to scream.

(*No answer.*)

I am. (*Pause.*) I'll scream till I get someone.

EDDIE: Scream away love, y'll only get me.

(VERA *hesitates. Then a tiny scream. No reaction from anyone. A louder scream. Nothing again. An even louder scream.*)

MARIE: Baybee . . . baybee . . .

(VERA *screams at the top of her voice.* MARIE *giggles.*)

VERA: I'm goin' to hang meself.

EDDIE: (*Gently*) Of course you are, and I'll hold on to your legs, now come on, you'll make yourself ill carryin' on like that.

(*He takes her and guides her past the padded cell and out.*)

MARIE: Baybee . . . baybeee . . . in lady's tummy, Petie. Petie.

PETE: She'd look daft with it in her shoe, wouldn't she?

MARIE: I'm goin' to get you after . . .

(CHRISTINE *comes back with a dazed* BEN. *She has hold of his arm and he is struggling half-heartedly. He is carrying a long slice of bacon.*)

BEN: No bloody wonder the bike wobbled. The wheel fell off.

CHRISTINE: Attempting two flights of stairs would see off most bikes, Ben.

BEN: The lift was being used.

CHRISTINE: So that's how you got it up here.

BEN: Shut up, you, woman, you know nothing. Worst thing they ever did, givin' you the vote. I was only three at the time but I knew then it was a mistake. And that soddin' Adam with his spare rib, he's got a lot to answer for, he has.

(CHRISTINE *sits him down as he talks. She attempts to take the bacon from him. He puts his hands behind his back and his feet in the air so that she can't get near him.*)

CHRISTINE: And where would we all be today if it hadn't been for Adam, hey?

BEN: (*Laughs. Becomes more and more agitated as the speech falls apart*) Where would we be? I'll tell you where we'd be – we'd be dead – dung and daisies – even better, never been born, seen the light of day, come out howling, huddled, smeared in blood, slipped on a seat at Lime Street, stowed on the bus for St Helens, left like a bomb for Barnardo's. 'Please take care of my son Ben. May God forgive me. Signed his loving mother.' One week old, sent to an orphanage, a home for housemasters to beat the buggery out of me, grow to be a man, masturbate, fornicate, marry, bring up my children, wish I'd put them on a bus t' St Helens, go grey, get old, bury my wife . . . should have burnt the bastard and her bile . . . but she left her daughters to burn me instead . . . to take good care of me, sign the forms, find the section, ooooh look, here we are, section 25, send f'the psychiatrist, send the senile old sod away, scrape him out of sight . . . Home from Home . . . Barnado's to Bedlam . . . Regan and Goneril . . . no Cordelia to die for me . . . just an abundance of fools around me in the last act . . . thank you, Adam. (*Goes to doff his cap.*) Thank you, spare ribs and chips, ninety-five pence.

CHRISTINE: I don't know half of what you're talking about most of the time, Ben, but if it's your daughters, you couldn't wish for better children . . . (*Tries to grab at his feet to take his shoes off, but he kicks out.*) . . . never miss a Sunday, neither of them . . . stop it . . . keep still . . . your bike-riding days are over . . . the distance they have to come and all . . . I've never heard such insults they have to put up with . . . you don't need your shoes for a start, come here . . .

(*He puts his feet behind his back as well as his hands.*)

BEN: I do need my shoes, I've got my old job back, doorman at the Cameo, got to be there at seven, there's a new film on, a follow up to Friar Tuck, called 'Try a Fu—'

CHRISTINE: Now that is enough from you, Ben Jacobs. (*But she stops struggling with him.*)

BEN: Jacobs, not even my own name, given to me at Barnado's, the first time they sent me to be adopted, the housemaster standing there saying, 'We're going to introduce you to the family as Jacobs because we all think you're crackers.' Only time I ever saw him laugh . . . now *he* was mad all right, smelt of malt whisky and armpits, had a great time in the First World War, the German Army's secret weapon, took his shirt off in the trenches, an' gassed a whole regiment.

(*He is so quiet now and docile that* CHRISTINE *moves away. He watches her go then sees* EDDIE *return alone.* EDDIE *and* CHRISTINE *go into the nurses' room.* BEN *takes one hand from behind his back, takes his shoe off. A small cigarette case and some loose change is in his shoe. He takes a cigarette out, finds matches in his pocket, lights a cigarette. Still has one hand behind his back.*)

EDDIE: Coffee?

CHRISTINE: No thanks. Could do with a ciggie though.

(*She sits down.* EDDIE *offers her a cigarette, but he has no matches.*)

My lighter's in my pocket.

(*She realizes, but* EDDIE *beats her to it, takes the coat, lifts it up, sees the cases, looks at* CHRISTINE, *fishes in her pocket, gets the lighter, lights her cigarette.*)

EDDIE: Suitcases? For an eight hour shift? (*Pause.*) Joinin' Peter on the road to Hawaii?

CHRISTINE: (*Looks at* EDDIE, *looks away.*) One of these days he really will go somewhere.

EDDIE: If he does, I'll have to go with him. I'd be lost without Barry Vincent after all these years.

CHRISTINE: He has me convinced some days.

EDDIE: And me. I am Barry Vincent. It is 1966, England will win the World Cup at Wembley this summer. I do share a room with him at C. F. Mott College of Education, I was born in Shoreditch. One day I will be a P.E. teacher. (*Half laughs, half snorts.*) D'you know what – told me so seriously the other night that I had a birth

mark on my chest, I was halfway to a mirror just to make sure.
(*Pause. They don't look at each other.*)
And where are *you* going?

CHRISTINE: What?

EDDIE: Come on love, you heard. Where are you going?

CHRISTINE: Who me?
(EDDIE *glares at her. She turns away, mumbles.*)
Don't know. (*Then firmer*) Not easy at my age, findin' somewhere . . . (*Smiles.*) At the Legion last Saturday . . . a dance, you know, well, Jimmy was behind the bar and then he was under the table . . . I had a few dances . . . two grown men told me they wished I was their mother . . .

EDDIE: Look, I've told you before, love, there's room with . . . well, with me.
(*She is not listening to him. He becomes aware of the fact.*)

CHRISTINE: Even leavin' in the first place . . . ironed him a shirt for tonight, made the bed . . .

EDDIE: Christine.

CHRISTINE: Actually found meself puttin' disinfectant down the toilet bowl . . .

EDDIE: Christine, listen, you're doing the best thing, don't you forget that. Remember what you said last year, the first time you ever talked about it.
(*She looks at him.*)
The Loony's Day Out.

CHRISTINE: (*Remembers. Smiles.*) On the chara . . .

EDDIE: Coming back from Southport. Marie's piddle runnin' right down the bus, Pete with a coat over his head on the back seat . . .

CHRISTINE: An' me up to here (*points to her brow*) in Bacardi. Yeah . . .

EDDIE: You know what you said. Once Carol's . . .

CHRISTINE: Left home. I know. And now she's left home . . . I just didn't think I'd be on me own so soon . . .

EDDIE: Leave a note?

(*She nods.*)

He'll find it when he comes home for his tea?

(*She nods again.*)

EDDIE: That'll make him happy.

(*She nods again.*)

What'll he do?

CHRISTINE: How the hell should I know? I've never left him before.

EDDIE: Come on, sod him, he's not worth it; by ten o'clock tonight we'll have the next twenty years all mapped out, me an' you. I can see it now, endin' up old and grey retired an' living in Morecambe, in the shadow of The Moby Dick, lookin' out across the estuary to . . .

CHRISTINE: I've dreamt of this y'know, for so long, slammin' the front door f'the last time . . . an' now that I've done it, I . . . don't feel any different. It doesn't seem no escape at all. (*She stubs her cigarette out. Brushes her uniform, as if about to stand.*)

EDDIE: But you know why, don't you?

(*She looks at him.*)

Because we're all creatures of habit.

CHRISTINE: (*Flatly*) Thanks Eddie, just what I need. You sound just like a psychiatrist.

EDDIE: (*Archly*) I'd be grateful if you didn't insult my intelligence, dear. (*He stands.*) One thing I've found out about psychiatrists, you only need one basic quality to be a psychiatrist. You have to be mad.

(EDDIE *goes out with a flourish, goes to the near doorway, takes a trolley with a teapot, half-a-dozen cups and plates of salad. He takes* MARIE *over to a seat at the table.*)

MARIE: (*As* EDDIE *gives her the salad*) I no want it, I no want it. I no like rabbit food. (*She pushes the plate away.*)

EDDIE: Come on darlin', just for me, there's a good girl.

MARIE: (*Loudly*) Marie no want it!

(EDDIE *puts the plate back in front of her.* CHRISTINE *comes out. Starts pouring tea.*)

EDDIE: For Eddie, go on there's a girl, just f'Eddie.

MARIE: Knickers to Eddie. (*A heavier push.*)

EDDIE: Now, now, Marie, who hasn't poo-pooed for three whole days?

MARIE: Teddy.

EDDIE: And Marie; now you and Teddy eat all our salad up and all your problems'll come to an end.

MARIE: No. Shan't.

(EDDIE *leans over and whispers to her. She looks up at him, looks at the salad, looks back at* EDDIE, *begins to eat.*)

EDDIE: There's my big girl. Come on, Ben, your tea's here, cock.

(*As soon as* EDDIE *turns his back on* MARIE *she rapidly puts the complete salad down her dress.*)

BEN: Boiled ham an' myxomatosis. I don't want it.

EDDIE: Suit y'self, but you'll not get anythin' else till breakfast.

BEN: (*As* EDDIE *turns away*) That's what you think: I've got somethin' up my sleeve.

(*Takes his hand from behind his back, making sure that* CHRISTINE *and* EDDIE *aren't looking. The tired-looking slice of bacon is in his hand. He wheezes and shakes with laughter.*)

EDDIE: Hey up, Peter, sittin' at the table?

PETE: No, Barry, not tonight, I'll stay where I am, no point in chancin' gettin' caught on me last night. Bring some back for me from the refectory if y' would. I've got a paper bag somewhere.

EDDIE: Y'can't go on like this y'know, lad.

PETE: I know, I'm runnin' out of paper bags. But I'm goin' tonight, Barry, tonight's the night.

(EDDIE *turns away. Goes towards the doorway of the nurses' room where* CHRISTINE *is standing. As he goes past* MARIE, *she shouts to him.*)

MARIE: All gone, Eddie, all in Marie's tummy. (*Holds her stomach*) Like lady's baby.

CHRISTINE: What did you say to Marie to make her eat?

EDDIE: I said I'd give her such an enema the bubbles'd come

out of her ears.

(EDDIE *goes to a cupboard and takes out a brown paper bag. Returns to the lounge. As he does so* VERA *re-enters. She has taken her coat off. Follows* EDDIE *as he goes to the table and watches as he lifts* PETE*'s plate and drops the food into the paper bag.* EDDIE *goes over to* PETE *and puts the bag at his side.* CHRISTINE *starts to organize the pills: opens the medicine cabinet, checks with a register what pills each patient should have. Not just for the ones in the lounge, but for the bed-ridden, etc.*)

PETE: Thanks, Barry.

(EDDIE *walks back to the table where* VERA *is standing.* MARIE *is focused on her stomach and* BEN *is watching her too.* EDDIE *moves a chair away from the table and motions to* VERA *to sit down at the side of* MARIE. *The plate of salad is in front of her.*)

VERA: I don't like salad.

EDDIE: The whole world doesn't like salad, Vera, but we have to keep the farmers happy, don't we?

(EDDIE *turns away and goes back towards the nurses' room. He begins his written daily report while* CHRISTINE *carries on sorting the pills out.* BEN *stands up and moves towards the table with his slice of bacon. Takes his meal from the other side of the table and moves his chair so he deliberately sits at* VERA*'s side so that her only way out is directly backwards. She has not seen the bacon in his hand. She picks at the boiled ham, fidgets, tries to move sideways away from* BEN, *is aware of the close proximity of both* BEN *and* MARIE. BEN *is staring at her face.* MARIE *is staring at her stomach.*)

BEN: Talkin' of farmers, this is interestin', y'll like this; I was fostered out to a farm once. In Wales. About ten of us there were. An' I hated the farmer's wife an' her stuck-up country ways. Declared war on her, I did. Used t'get up in the middle of the night and go down the yard and milk buggery out of her cows, open all her gates an' scare the shit out of her sheep. Tight-arsed old twat she was an' all – typical woman now that I think about it – porridge f'breakfast every day – same as she give the pigs – an' then of a Sunday, one rasher of streaky bacon and an egg the size of a marble. Well, this is the best bit, tickle you this will; one Sunday mornin' I got up before everyone else, knocked back my bacon an' egg, then stuck the rind up me nose. An' then when all the others came down f'breakfast I kept tellin' them how bad the bacon was, an' how they shouldn't touch it. An' then just as they started to tuck in, I started coughin' an' splutterin' an' then I fetched a massive big piece of rind from down me nostril as proof the bacon was off . . .

(VERA *pushes the plate further away from herself, goes to leave, but* BEN *moves his chair in towards hers.*)

. . . an' then, an' then they all turned green an' pushed the bacon away, an' when they'd all gone I ate it all, every last piece. (*Pause.*) Funny thing that was, the bacon really was off. I was sick for days.

MARIE: Hey, Ben, look what Marie did, look, look . . . (*She laughs and pulls out from the top of her dress the lettuce leaves, radish, etc., then finally a piece of boiled ham.*)

BEN: (*Looks at Vera's plate, looks at her, sees her revulsion. Produces the slice of bacon.*) D'you want this, do you? Hey? Go nice with that. (*Dangles it in front of her.*) Feel it, go on, feel it, it's all right, it's dead . . .

MARIE: I can't find the tomato. (*Pats herself, looks underneath the chair*) Don't tell Eddie, don't tell him, Ben.

(*As she comes up,* VERA *has stood up, and* MARIE'*s face is at her stomach level.* MARIE *leans across to grab hold of* BEN, *sees how near she is to* VERA'*s stomach.*)

Baybee . . . baybee . . .

(MARIE *puts her hand out and also tries to rest her head on* VERA'*s stomach.* VERA *turns quickly away, straight into* BEN *who has stood up as well.*)

BEN: (*Still dangling the bacon*) Know what sucking pig is, do you, girl? Ever tasted it, have you? Don't get that in a box from the Co-op, I'll tell you. Baby pig, that's what it is – torn straight off some poor sow's nipple. Throat cut, warmed up an' thrown on a plate.

(MARIE, *during this speech, must begin to be upset by it too, as if a memory, long drowned, is coming back to her.*)

When you have your baby, woman, kill it, d'you hear, kill it, cut its throat on the operating table! (*He spits the last words into her face.*)

VERA: Jesus Christ, it's a madhouse in here!

(*She stumbles away from the table, pushing blindly at* BEN, *knocking her chair over. She cries out.* EDDIE *and* CHRISTINE *rush out of their room.* CHRISTINE *goes over to* VERA. *Holds her, guides her, near hysterical, towards where* EDDIE *is standing coldly watching.* BEN *has hustled away from the table, sat down, put the bacon down the side of his chair.*)

MARIE: (*Very quietly*) Operating table . . .

VERA: I wanna go home, I wanna go home.

CHRISTINE: Now, now, love, you've only just arrived, everything's always takes a bit of gettin' used to at first . . .

VERA: (*Laughs wildly.*) Christ, I'll never get used to this. I was better off at home with the kids . . .

CHRISTINE: Come on, have a little rest . . . good night's sle—

VERA: I just want to be on my own . . .

EDDIE: Oh dear, not another Greta Garbo, that'll be four we've got now. Plus two Marlon Brandos, three Norman Tebbits and a whole ward full of Arthur Scargills.

VERA: I'm goin' to report you, you're supposed t'be here to help!

EDDIE: That's right, help those who can't help themselves, not holidaymakers an' tourists.

VERA: I don't have to stay here y'know, you can't stop me, I'm goin' t'sign meself out.

EDDIE: (*Takes a pen out of his pocket.*) Here you are, sign away, the papers are in the office, we even give you the bus fare home.

(EDDIE *turns away towards the nurses' room.* VERA *looks away.* BEN *turns and cackles,* VERA *flares up, rushes over to* BEN *before* CHRISTINE *can stop her. She manages to half hit him over the top of his head. He goes into a ball in the easy chair.*)

VERA: You won't be laughin' when my feller comes on Sunday, you won't, y'old bastard.

(CHRISTINE *takes* VERA *away from* BEN *towards another chair. As soon as she sits down,* BEN *cackles again.* CHRISTINE *turns angrily towards him. He stops in mid-cackle, straight-faced.* CHRISTINE *draws a chair up beside* VERA.)

CHRISTINE: Now come on, Vera, tell me what happened.

VERA: It was him, old as he is, I'll still . . .

CHRISTINE: Yes all right, but what did he do?

VERA: It was horrible. And her too. (*Points at* MARIE, *who is lost to the world.*) The pair of them. (*Looks towards the nurses' room.*) An' I don't care what that pineapple in there says, I am y'know, I'm sick. Me nerves were in such a state I couldn't talk to no one – like I was in a sort of y'know capsule – like the soddin' pills they give y' – all wrapped up. In meself. The kids . . . Jeez, the kids . . . got to the stage where the nappies used to be so embarrassed they changed themselves. (*Laughs. A mixture of bravery and self-pity.*)

CHRISTINE: How many children have you got, Vera?

VERA: Three. Three, two an' one, they are. (*Points to her stomach.*) An' this one in here. Makes four. An annual event, like the Whit Walks.

CHRISTINE: You don't look old enough. (CHRISTINE *offers her a cigarette.*)

VERA: I'm twenty-two. Next birthday. If I make it that far.

CHRISTINE: (*Without too much conviction*) Oh come on, don't be silly, there's many people much worse off than you.

VERA: Yeah, in the Amazon. Or in here.

CHRISTINE: What about your husband?

VERA: It's not me feller, y'know; not because of him I'm

here. Lot of women, I know, they're here 'cos of their husbands an' what they've done to them. Our Joan, she was here, that was the trouble with her. The swine; used her like a dustbin he did. Take anythin' our Joan. But my Dave, do anythin' to make me happy, he would. Anythin'. Near in tears he was when he took the kids to me Mam's this afternoon. (*Pause.*) It's just that lately he's, well, he's had a lot of overtime, every bloody night near enough, he's workin' . . . it gets y'down y'know, . . . I mean, it's fair enough, he's doin' it for me, I know that . . . (*Brightens.*) . . . We're savin' for a house of our own, y'see, that's what Dave says all the overtime's for, I never see a penny of it, puts it all in the bank every month, Dave does. It won't be long now, we'll have a house of our own . . .

CHRISTINE: (*Pats her arm, stands.*) There you are love, something to look forward to. Not everyone's got something to look forward to, you know. You'll soon sort yourself out, you will.

(*She moves away from* VERA, *who seems not to notice.* CHRISTINE *approaches* PETE, *who is painting. She stands above him.*)

Good that, Peter.

PETE: I know.

CHRISTINE: Another picture of Hawaii.

(*He nods.*)

Are you really going to go there?

PETE: (*Carries on painting after only the slightest of pauses.*) 'Course I am; but don't tell anyone . . . ever since I can remember I've wanted to go there. The only postcard me Dad ever wrote to me, he wrote from Hawaii. I took it to school and me teacher put it up on the noticeboard for the whole school to see. My Dad's letter to me. An' some thievin' twat went an' stole it.

(CHRISTINE *puts her hand gently on* PETE's *shoulder. He carries on painting and she moves away, back to the nurses' room where* EDDIE *is.*)

EDDIE: What was all that about with Vera?

CHRISTINE: She wouldn't say, but it was obviously something to do with Ben.

EDDIE: He should have ridden that bike under a bus – put us all out of our misery. Still an' all, can't help likin' the mad old bugger.

CHRISTINE: It might be an idea to start likin' Vera . . .

EDDIE: Look, no offence meant, Christine, but you've only been here, what – two and a half years? – I've been here since Adam was a lad, and I've seen too many of her kind. Done a lot of good, the Mental Health Act, but along with the good y've got the layabouts who are just swinging the lead, having a rest from their responsibilities. And as soon as their Social Security drops down, they've signed themselves out. When we first started gettin' them I believed the first few, but now, if they haven't taken two hundred phenobarbitone in the first week I throw them out.

CHRISTINE: Well, from what she's just been telling me, I feel sorry for her.

EDDIE: You would do though, wouldn't you? I've seen you crying over that rubbish on the telly. You even got upset over one of the commercials – and I told you he'd come back to her when she cleaned her teeth.

CHRISTINE: (*Pushes him.*) Oh go away!

EDDIE: No, I can remember the time, when I first started, all we had then was the violent and the criminally insane. None of these with bad nerves an' trouble with the gas bill. Had to book in advance for the padded cell. No treatment like there is these days. No therapy or facilities or end in sight then. Keep them locked away like lepers, that's what we had to do. Much better now, all things considered, but there was some good times then as well. All my mates in here were murderers an' sex maniacs – had a way with them, I did – grew old with them as well. Most of them dead now of course, yet they never gave me any problems I couldn't cope with. Had more respect an' understanding for them than . . .

CHRISTINE: The likes of Vera?

EDDIE: Aye.

CHRISTINE: But Eddie, anyone who comes in here must be, in some way . . .

EDDIE: Mad? Perhaps. But for every one of that kind who's genuine, y'get a load more treatin' us like a caravan site. (*Stands.*) Marie's quiet tonight – have you noticed? She's usually the life an' soul of the party after she's been in there.

CHRISTINE: It's probably the sight of someone new – pregnant and all.

EDDIE: I know – my first thoughts.

(*They go back into the lounge during the following scene and start to collect the dinner plates, cups, etc. Put them on the trolley. Not too careful about being heard by the patients, apart from* VERA.)

CHRISTINE: Anything new always upsets them.

EDDIE: Like children, seein' a new face for the first time. Young Peter terrified of Jaws when I first brought it in for him . . .

CHRISTINE: Only because Ben told him it was an orange-coloured piranha.

EDDIE: Mind you, it's not just them. Most of us are frightened of something. We are though, aren't we? I mean, me, I can't bear the touch of worms. And you, Christine, what are you frightened of?

CHRISTINE: (*Pause.*) You're about as subtle as a sewerage farm at times, aren't you, Eddie? (*Turns away from him.*)

EDDIE: It's just sort of . . . my way of offerin' my services.

CHRISTINE: What services would they be, then? What have you got to offer?

EDDIE: Peace and quiet . . . affection . . . warmth.

CHRISTINE: (*Looks around herself.*) Where are the violins? I had affection and warmth from the kids, till they left. And I get peace and quiet when he's at the Legion. I have to laugh. He had flat feet when he tried to join up for Malaya.

EDDIE: Huh. Don't mention that to me.

CHRISTINE: Flat feet?

EDDIE: Malaya.

CHRISTINE: Were you in Malaya?

EDDIE: I thought I told you not to mention that particular part of Indonesia.

CHRISTINE: What happened?

EDDIE: Where?

CHRISTINE: In Malaya.

EDDIE: There you go again. Mentioning Malaya. (*She laughs.*) Put it this way, chuck, I was a prisoner of war – and I never once saw the enemy.

CHRISTINE: I don't understand you.

EDDIE: (*With an edge*) Neither did they.

CHRISTINE: But what do you mean, Eddie?

EDDIE: Oh nothing. Just nothing.

CHRISTINE: Were you wounded?

EDDIE: Stabbed in the back as it were . . . But listen, if you're worried about somewhere to go, y'know, I've told you, my place is free. One thing for certain, I won't be carrying any thoughts of anyone else around with me . . .

CHRISTINE: (*Gently*) Man, woman or beast.

EDDIE: I know what people say . . . behind my back . . . but I'm not . . .

CHRISTINE: Right now, Eddie love, I couldn't care less if the romance of your life'd been Dick the Donkey under the Pier at Blackpool.

EDDIE: So you'll come then?

CHRISTINE: Well . . .

(*All the plates, etc., from tea are on the trolley.* EDDIE *has hold of the trolley, starts pushing it towards the doors by the cell.*)

EDDIE: Right, I'll put these outside and go and check Mountbatten – a new auxiliary on there – caught her sterilizin' spoons in a bedpan on Tuesday . . . (*Gets to the door.*)

PETE: Barry, Barry!

EDDIE: Going for a run, Peter, big match on Saturday, got to be fit, y'know.

(*Off.* CHRISTINE *looks at* MARIE, BEN *and* VERA. *Totally separated. No communication.*)

PETE: Good footballer y'know, Barry. Plays in the first team.

CHRISTINE: I bet he isn't as good as you though, Peter.

PETE: He's better than me. At everythin'. (*Said with no suggestion of self-pity.*) Including pullin' women. Locks me out of his room when he's at it. One of them, Sylvia someone . . .

CHRISTINE: Right, anyone want to play anything? Draughts, whist, dominoes?

MARIE: Doctors an' nurses.

VERA: Have y'got anythin' to read?

CHRISTINE: There's some books and magazines in my room, I'll go and fetch them.

(*She walks through the lounge. The phone rings. Loudly. She looks at her watch. Gets to the door, hesitates, picks up the phone nervously.*)

Churchill . . . Oh, it's you, Freda . . . what's it been like over there, we've been a bit hectic . . .

BEN: I've got just the book for you, I have y'know.

VERA: I don't want to read it.

BEN: (*Off his chair and on his haunches*) Suit you down to the ground. (*Pause.*) Well, halfway down t'the ground anyway. (*He giggles.*)

VERA: The nurse is gettin' me some books.

BEN: She won't get you this one, it's mine, but I'll let you have a lend of it . . . if you ask me nicely.

VERA: I don't want it, whatever it is. Go away before I . . .

BEN: It's called *Rosemary's Baby*, but we can easily change the title f'you.

MARIE: (*Distantly*) Rosemary's baybee . . .

VERA: Go away, just go away, I'm warning you . . .

MARIE: Marie's baybee . . .

BEN: It's all about this woman, this book, *Rosemary's Baby*. Her name was Rosemary see, an' she had a baby . . .
MARIE: Marie had a baby . . .
BEN: But it was no ordinary common or garden baby – not the kind of baby y'could lose between Lime Street an' St Helens, not without there bein' consequences . . .
VERA: I'll call the nurse . . .
BEN: It was the devil's baby.
MARIE: Oooooh! (*Stands with her teddy, goes over towards* BEN *and* VERA.)
BEN: That's what it was . . . she had a hell of a time with it, y'know . . . (*Giggles.*) . . . the pains she had, as if there were red hot coals in her stomach . . .
(CHRISTINE *puts the phone down. Goes to the cupboard to get the books.*)
. . . an' then when it was ready to burst like a pea in a pod . . .
VERA: Nurse . . . nurse . . .
MARIE: Marie's baby . . .
BEN: That was a bad time that was . . . poor Rosemary . . .
MARIE: Poor Marie . . .
BEN: The little devil was born with horns . . . can y' imagine . . . ripped the insides out of her, clean out . . .
MARIE: (*Suddenly hitting* BEN *hard with her teddy*) No, no, no, it never . . .
VERA: *Nurse!*
CHRISTINE: Oh Christ! (*Drops the books, comes rushing out.* BEN *scuttles away from* VERA, *back to his chair, holds his head, sits stone-faced.*)
VERA: It's him, nurse, it's him again, he's mad.
CHRISTINE: I am warning you, Ben, I really am. You've been nothing but a pain in the arse all bloody night long.
BEN: Just like Rosemary's Baby. (*He shakes with silent laughter.*)
CHRISTINE: It won't be a joke where we send you.
BEN: I was only askin' her somethin'.
VERA: No he wasn't.

BEN: They ganged up on me.

VERA: He was tryin' to scare me.

BEN: An' I did an' all.

CHRISTINE: Come Monday mornin', you're goin' to be the one who's scared, Ben Jacobs, mark my words.

BEN: You're not sendin' me t'get practised on by that electrician's mate down there.

CHRISTINE: I am that.

BEN: You're not 'cos you don't make any decisions around here, you're just a woman. Your job's to empty the piss pots.

(EDDIE *arrives back in. Witnesses the disintegration of* BEN*'s speech, sees him rise, fists pathetically raised.*)

Please the patients, bath the babies, fetch an' bring it, give birth an' bury it, leave out the milk bottles, take in the milkman . . . you woman, you tumour, you disease!

(EDDIE *grabs hold of him from behind, holds him tightly.* BEN *seems to sag into his arms.*)

EDDIE: You stupid old bugger, gettin' everyone upset.

BEN: I was not.

EDDIE: 'Course you bloody well was – I heard you – daft as a brush you are sometimes. An educated man like you, and all.

BEN: Self-educated.

EDDIE: Even more to be proud of, instead of . . .

BEN: I was only talkin' to the new infection . . .

EDDIE: See what I mean?

VERA: You were tellin' me about *Rosemary's Baby*, you evil old sod. Puttin' the fear of God into me, and the state I'm in.

MARIE: He give Marie bad memories.

VERA: My feller'll hear about this, I'm not tellin' no lies – he'll soon sort you out.

EDDIE: Any sorting out to be done, I'll do it, no one else.

VERA: You? You couldn't sort out my make-up case. It takes a man not a paper tissue.

CHRISTINE: (*Going to* VERA) I've told Ben, any more and it's down to ECT on Monday. (*She takes* VERA *away, back to the chair, gives her the magazine she still has.*)

EDDIE: Did you hear that, cock? Did you hear what nurse said then?

BEN: She hasn't got no power.

EDDIE: But you will have on Monday hey, won't you? (*A quiet friendly delivery*) That's right, isn't it? Full of power you'll be then, won't you? First thing Monday mornin', get you ready, put on your nice new dressing gown, take you down, strap you in place, wire you up, plug you in, all those lovely shiny electrodes; might even forget to give you a general – like when I first started – no anaesthetics in those days y'know – bones breakin' all over the place – old feller like you, brittle as honeycomb, dose of Manweb goin' through you, might just heal your mind an' break your body . . .

BEN: (*Stares at him, visibly subdued*) Y'wouldn't.

EDDIE: Why wouldn't I? Just like everyone else I am, y'know Ben. Like a bit of peace an' quiet now an' then, only fair . . .

BEN: Y'worse than her, you are. Wha've you got down there – a fanny? (*Half-hearted attempt to feel* EDDIE'*s privates.*)

EDDIE: No, but you'll have an electric organ on Monday, my lad, Reginald Dixon, that's who you'll be. They'll put so many volts through you, you'll get Luxemburg and VHF never mind Radio One. (*Takes him and practically lifts him into a chair.*) Now one more peep before bed an' we'll be cookin' the dinner on you all next week . . . (EDDIE *turns around, looks at everyone.* PETE *seemingly untouched by all that has gone on,* MARIE *slumped into her chair with her teddy over her face,* CHRISTINE *talking to* VERA. *He turns and walks back to the nurses' room.* PETE *watches him till he turns into the room.*)

VERA: Listen, isn't there anywhere else I could go in here? I mean, do I have t'be stuck with this lot? It's not safe in here . . .

CHRISTINE: You weren't expected . . . no room elsewhere.

VERA: I came past an empty ward on my way up here.

CHRISTINE: Government cuts, lack of money, lousy wages, shortage of staff. Psychiatric nurses are hard to find.

VERA: An' I haven't found one now, have I?

CHRISTINE: The only trouble with Eddie is that he can't get used to seein' what he thinks are normal people in here. (*She stands up.*)

VERA: *I'm* normal.

CHRISTINE: So, what are you doing in here then?

VERA: I'm just temporary sick, that's all. My doctor explained it to me. He said you can be mentally sick for a time and then get better – same as havin' an ulcer or a broken leg or somethin' – that you're not really a loony or nothin'. But you've got to have treatment, same as if y' were physically sick.

CHRISTINE: Well, you try telling Eddie and the rest of the old brigade that, and see what sort of an answer you get. (CHRISTINE *leaves* VERA *and walks back to the nurses' room, where* EDDIE *is putting the pills on a tray, ready to give out.*)

EDDIE: Vera been entertainin' you again with all her sorrows, has she? The binmen missed her out an' she had a crack-up? Or was it the telly broke an' she couldn't cope?

CHRISTINE: She's in a bigger mess than you'll ever let yourself find out.

EDDIE: People like her, they make their bed, should learn t'lie in it, instead of runnin' away . . . (*He realizes what he has said.*)

CHRISTINE: That includes me as well, hey, Eddie? I'm runnin' away.

EDDIE: You're runnin' away to what y'hope is somewhere better. You've served your time in hell, the likes of Vera haven't even hit purgatory yet.

CHRISTINE: There'll be more than purgatory hit when he finds that note. (*Looks at her watch.*) Just leavin' the Legion he'll be now. Five minutes an' he'll be in the house. Look out world!

EDDIE: Does . . . I mean, d'y'think he might . . . come here?

CHRISTINE: You'll be all right, Eddie. After all, you're used to real madmen, aren't you?

EDDIE: But I've never had it in mind to take one of their wives home before.

CHRISTINE: But that's the funny thing, Eddie – he's been waiting for me to run off with the man from the Pru for the past twenty years. And I've never been unfaithful to him once.

EDDIE: I'm not asking you to be unfaithful, I'm just asking you to come home with me. (*Pause.*)

CHRISTINE: I'm going to need somewhere. At least for tonight.

EDDIE: I knew I should have changed the sheets. Last year.

(*They both reach out for the tray of pills at the same time. Both embarrassed at being near to each other.*)

CHRISTINE: I'll take the water.

(*She picks a jug and some small glasses up on a tray. They both go into the lounge.* CHRISTINE *takes* MARIE'*s and* BEN'*s pills over to them. They take theirs without comment or even seeming to notice.* EDDIE *approaches* PETE. PETE *shakes his head.*)

EDDIE: Now come on, Peter, good for standin' on the M62 these pills are. Make you nice and relaxed – keeps your thumb up as well. Not get any lifts with a collapsed thumb y'know.

PETE: I don't want any. They make you feel tired. Your thumb an' all.

EDDIE: Come 'head, lad, no messing around now.

PETE: No. Don't want to.

EDDIE: Look, everyone else's havin' theirs.

PETE: They're not goin' to Hawaii tonight. I am.

EDDIE: (*For the first time losing his temper*) F'God's sake, Peter, I've got enough to think about right now. You couldn't even make it to Woolies for y'passport picture . . . now are you going to take this tablet or not?

PETE: But . . . but . . . I can't . . . an' I've got a ten-year passport.

EDDIE: Right. (*Goes towards the doorway by the nurses' room.*)

PETE: Barry . . . Barry, where y'goin'? Don't leave me, *Barry*.

(PETE *gets up, knocking his water over again, runs stiffly towards* EDDIE.)

EDDIE: (*Gently, putting his free arm around him*) I am going down to the bed-ridden with their tablets, Peter. For the past God knows how many years I've done that at seven o'clock, as you well know. But remember this, kidder, if that tablet isn't inside you when I get back, Nurse Matthews will hold you down and I'll find some place for it to go.

PETE: (*Desperately*) No, look, look, I'll take it now look, see! (*Brings* EDDIE *back a pace or two, puts the tablet into his mouth, makes exaggerated gestures.*) Yummy, yummy, yummy, nice, all gone, see. (*Holds his mouth open.* EDDIE *has already gone.*) You will come back, won't you. Barry?

(PETE *comes back towards the centre of the lounge.* CHRISTINE *watches him. He looks at her out of the corner of his eye, looks back at her, she is no longer watching him. He takes the tablet from under his tongue triumphantly, then panics, looks at* CHRISTINE *and all the others. No one has seen him. He then steps in the spilt water in his bare feet. Stays there, looking down, moaning slightly, until* CHRISTINE *comes over.*)

CHRISTINE: Helpless as a cripple with fleas, you are, aren't you? Come here. (*Takes hold of his hand – the one with the tablet. He keeps it clenched.*)

PETE: I er . . . want some water. I've got to have some water. Honest. Right now.

CHRISTINE: I thought you might. (*Goes over to the jug, sees that it is empty.*) We could do with a tap just for you in here.

(*She looks around at everyone.* VERA *sitting still smoking a cigarette staring at* BEN, MARIE *with her teddy.* BEN *with his hands underneath himself.* CHRISTINE *takes* PETE'S cup and follows after EDDIE. *As soon as she goes,* VERA *stands and comes over to* BEN, *stands directly in front of him. He glances up at her, then quickly down. She grabs him by the hair so that he has to look at her.*)

VERA: I've sat here, thinkin' about you, just thinkin', sittin' there, thinkin', about what you did before, you thought it was clever, didn't you? Think y' scared me, well, where I come from, we know what t'do with the likes of you, an' I'll see it done an' all, however old or daft you are . . .

(MARIE *leans forward, laughs nervously.* PETE *comes over to* VERA.)

PETE: Look, I never took my tablet, look. (*He is ignored.*)

MARIE: Smack him, go on, smack him, he's been a naughty boy.

BEN: Y' not gettin' me into trouble, I'm not goin' down t'the sparks on Monday.

MARIE: Get him, go on, get him, stick a hat-pin in him.

BEN: (*Fast, excited*) She's not wearin' a hat. (*Giggles, stops abruptly.*)

VERA: Enjoy yourself, go ahead, I'll fix you before I leave here. (*Pushes him.*)

MARIE: (*Excited too*) An' I'm goin' to get Petie tomorrow, aren't I, Petie? Me an' the others. Y'can join in if you want, lady.

PETE: Y'won't 'cos I haven't taken my pill. (*Holds his pill up.*) I'll be on a boat to Hawaii tomorrow, me an' Jaws!

BEN: (*As* VERA *releases her grip on him after pushing him – straight at her, with the venom of the earlier speeches*) I knew someone went to Hawaii once, a woman, went on a cattle boat. (*Laughs sharply.*) Stayed out there, so I heard tell, met a fool an' married him, had a child an' all, a lovely baby boy, loved that child with all her heart she did, always made sure she took him off the bus with her, played with him all the time, bouncin' him an' throwin' him up an' catching him, an' the baby gurgled an' giggled an' laughed, an' the more she threw him up an' the higher she threw him up, the more he laughed an' giggled an' gurgled, an' then, one fine day, she threw him higher than she'd ever thrown him before, an' she put his head right through the electric fan that it is the custom to have on the ceilings in these hot countries, an' it went whirr whirr whirr around and around an' as she held her hands out to catch him, he came down in slices, slices, *slices*!

(*He takes the slice of bacon from behind his back and waves it in* VERA*'s face. She screams and knocks it out of his hand. She runs away from him towards the dinner table.* MARIE *picks up the slice of bacon, holds it in her arms, as if cradling it.*)

VERA: Nurse, nurse, *NURSE!*

MARIE: Baybee, poor baybee.

(PETE *turns away from them and towards the fish tank, drops the pill in the tank.*)

PETE: We're going to Hawaii tonight, me an' you, Jaws. Best get some sleep for a few . . . (*Looks at the tank more carefully.*) Jaws . . . Jaws . . . someone's murdered him . . . someone's killed my goldfish. (*Sees the empty pepperpot. Turns to* BEN.) It was you, you killed him!

(PETE *goes over to* BEN, *makes awkward attempts at violence. Never actually hits him, always stops, but finally kicks* BEN*'s shins and runs away.*)

BEN: Nurse, nurse, *NURSE!*

(MARIE *goes over to where* VERA *is huddled on a chair, and very gently places the slice of bacon on her stomach.* VERA *goes hysterical as soon as she sees it.* CHRISTINE *comes running in, spilling water.* EDDIE *races in seconds after her.* EDDIE *goes over to* PETE *who is still making punching actions into thin air. He takes hold of his arms.*)

MARIE: Better now, baybee.

(CHRISTINE *takes the bacon off* VERA*'s stomach. She is still hysterical. As she stands up, the phone rings loudly in the nurses' room.* VERA *pushes* CHRISTINE *away from her* *and runs towards the opposite doors.* CHRISTINE *starts to follow her. The phone continues to ring.*)

CHRISTINE: Vera. Vera!

PETE: (*Turning to* EDDIE, *blocking his vision of* CHRISTINE) Ben done my goldfish in. He poisoned Jaws.

(CHRISTINE *goes towards the phone.* MARIE *follows after her as* EDDIE *forces* PETE *away from both* BEN *and the goldfish tank.*)

MARIE: Nurse, nurse . . .

(CHRISTINE *gets to the phone. Picks it up. She winces, listens briefly, holds the phone away from her.* MARIE *is alongside her. More coherent than before. She holds on to Christine's sleeve.*)

I lost my baby once, nurse, I lost mine too. Just like that lady. It was a long time ago, I lost my little baby . . . but I never got to play with him even . . . I never made him gurgle . . . I never did none of those things . . . I never held him, never fed him or burped him or threw him too high . . . none of them . . . I want my baby back . . . give me my baby back . . . (*She kneels down on the floor and sobs on* CHRISTINE*'s knee. The phone is still hanging loosely in* CHRISTINE*'s hand at her side.* MARIE *can hear her husband's voice. She leans across, screams down the phone.*)

I want my baby back!

(CHRISTINE *takes the phone away from her.*)

CHRISTINE: That's what he wants and all, love. (*She drops the phone back on the hook. Puts her arm around* MARIE. *Starts singing.*)

'Rocky-a-bye baby on the tree top
When the wind blows the cradle will rock,
When the bough breaks the cradle will fall,
Down will come cradle, baby and all . . .'

(*The phone starts ringing again as the lights go slowly down.* CHRISTINE *just stares at it.*)

Darkness.

A phone ringing loudly, on Christine's desk.

Lights up. CHRISTINE *sitting there watching the phone. We see her pick the phone up, hold it away from herself for a second, then drop it down. Sits there.*

BEN, MARIE, PETE *in the lounge with* EDDIE. BEN *staring,* PETE *looking at a large map of the world.* EDDIE *is doing* MARIE*'s hair, fixing her ribbons, putting slide in. She has a mirror and is looking at herself. As soon as* CHRISTINE *drops the phone,* EDDIE *starts singing quietly.*

EDDIE: 'Who is that pretty girl in the mirror there?
What mirror where? . . .'

MARIE: It's me.

EDDIE: Get-away, it's not is it? (*Looks at her, looks in the mirror*) So it is, well well well. Who'd believe it?
(*The phone starts ringing again.* EDDIE *glances across.*)

MARIE: Phone's ringing again.

EDDIE: Yes, I can hear it.

MARIE: It stops if you pick it up.

EDDIE: Not this one dear, I'm afraid.

MARIE: It does, Marie show you.
(*She goes to get up.* EDDIE *puts his hand on her shoulder.*)

EDDIE: Will madame kindly be seated? Pierre has not yet completed his creation.
(*We see* CHRISTINE *pick up the phone again. Drop it again.*)

MARIE: Phone stopped.

EDDIE: Thank you, madame, now sit ever so still or monsieur's reputation will be in ruins.

MARIE: What're you talkin' all funny for?

EDDIE: I am pretending to be a hairdresser, madame.

BEN: Pretendin's the right word an' all. Seen better heads on a mop.

EDDIE: Thank you, Ben, your charm will not go unrewarded.
(*Phone starts again.*)

MARIE: Phone started again.

EDDIE: I know, I know . . . just excuse me one moment, Madame . . .

(*Three paces and* CHRISTINE *picks it up, drops it again.*)

MARIE: It's stopped, Eddie.

(EDDIE *comes back, stands behind* MARIE.)

Listen, it's not there.

(EDDIE *mimes strangling her. She sees him in the mirror, turns around.*)

I saw you, I saw you! You strangle me an' I'll tell a policeman, I will.

(*The phone rings again.*)

EDDIE: Oh sufferin' Christ! (*He goes towards the nurses' room.*)

PETE: Barry . . .

(EDDIE *goes straight past him.*)

. . . Thanks for the map . . . but it hasn't got Sheffield on it . . . Barry.

EDDIE: Are you goin' to answer it?

CHRISTINE: (*Picks up the phone, drops it again.*) What's the point?

EDDIE: The point is that he has been phoning here for over an hour now, non-bloody-stop, we're not allowed to take the phone off the hook, you've got to talk to him sooner or later.

CHRISTINE: I will talk to him, but not now. I tried before; couldn't get a word in edgeways.

EDDIE: Some fun we're goin' to have tonight.

CHRISTINE: Well, next time he rings, you answer it.

EDDIE: Me? He only wants to break every bone in my body – it's you he really wants.

CHRISTINE: You shouldn't have told him who you were.

EDDIE: It was the way he asked me. (*Deep voice*) 'Are you that queer-arsed queen they call Eddie?' (*Pause.*) And anyway, what have you been saying about me?

CHRISTINE: Y'know how jealous he is. I just thought it was better, that's all, if he thought . . .

EDDIE: Well, I'm not, d'y'hear me, Christine. Not. And

never have been and never will be.
(*The phone rings again.* EDDIE *grabs it.*)
Yes this is the queer-arsed queen they call Eddie . . . Oh sorry Matron, what . . . oh nothin' . . . a joke . . . yes . . . that's right . . . the phone has been busy. No, really, it hasn't been off the hook, we've just been . . . busy. (*Listens, puts his hand over the phone.*) They've picked Vera up . . . Is she, matron? Yes, she was somewhat distressed when she left here too . . . All right yes, we'll have her, give us a ring when . . . on second thoughts, I'll come down in about twenty minutes, all right? (*Puts the phone down.*)

CHRISTINE: In a state?

EDDIE: Vera? Apparently. Hardly surprisin', really.

CHRISTINE: Look, I'm sorry . . .

EDDIE: So am I. Just the pressure . . . you know . . . like a bloody battlefield in here tonight. D'you know what I've done in the last hour and a half? Held Marie down an' sedated her, for what that was worth after twenty-odd years of it, took a slide out of Hettie Tinsley's hair when she was asleep, wrapped it up in Christmas paper f'Marie, took Peter's goldfish out . . .
(*The phone rings.* EDDIE *picks it up for a second, drops it down again.*) . . . took Peter's goldfish out an' buried it, diggin' a soddin' hole in the lawn with a dessert spoon, him watchin' me out of the window, complainin' 'cos he wanted him cremated, broke into the Library Room an' took the map of the world off the wall, put out an alert f'Vera . . .
(*Phone rings.*)
(*Chinese accent*) Hello, Wong's Chinese Takeaway . . . (*Puts the phone down.*) . . . took Ben for a walk past ECT, made Peter a black armband an' combed Marie's hair. I should be in about twenty-nine different unions f'that, from hairdressers to gravediggers. Now don't just sit there – do something, right?
(*The phone rings.*)

Like answering the phone and getting it over with.
(*The phone rings for some seconds. Then* CHRISTINE *picks it up.*)

CHRISTINE: Yes, Jimmy.
(EDDIE *puts his arm around her shoulder briefly, then goes out, back into the lounge.* MARIE *is still sitting with her mirrors.*)

EDDIE: Oh, madame! Almost perfection. From the rear, well, it simply has to be seen to be believed. Just a little touch here, perhaps? (*He fusses with her hair at the back, briefly.*)

CHRISTINE: Y'wastin' your time.

EDDIE: And here? (*Finishes. Lifts her hands up with the mirror to see both sides.*)

CHRISTINE: Y'shouldn't have bothered. There's no point.

EDDIE: C'est magnifique! Shampoo and set tomorrow, hey Marie? The old Twink Special? What do you say? Me an' you?

CHRISTINE: No, *no one else.* Just enough of you, Jimmy.
(MARIE, *as* CHRISTINE *talks, holds the mirror in her lap and looks down at herself. Spits on the mirror – a child's careful spit – no force. Wipes the spit all around the mirror. Then a little spit in a corner.*)

EDDIE: Really, madame, such compliments are rare.

MARIE: Phone stopped again, Eddie.

EDDIE: Yes, so it has.

MARIE: I like making phone calls.

EDDIE: I know you do, dear. We all know you like making phone calls. Every police officer, fireman and ambulance driver in Merseyside knows all about your phone calls.
(MARIE *fusses briefly with her hair.*)

CHRISTINE: If you're going to carry on like that, I'm putting the phone down.

MARIE: It's nice, talking to someone. On the phone.

EDDIE: Of course it is. Mr Richard Soles of Sefton Park just loves listening to you. 'Is that Richard Soles, is it?' (*High-pitched voice*) 'R. Soles, R. Soles, R. Soles.'

MARIE: P. Nutt.

EDDIE: Pardon?

MARIE: Three P. Nutts. In the book. (*Giggles.*) One even lives in Almond Drive.

EDDIE: Just you dare, Marie Webster. Just you bloody well dare. I had enough trouble with R. So— Mr Soles.

MARIE: I want some lipstick and make-up.

CHRISTINE: There's no point.

EDDIE: Oh aye? Goin' out, are you? Got a date?

BEN: (*Suddenly, quickly*) Les Behan.

MARIE: I'm not.

BEN: Maths teacher at my last school. Name of Leslie Behan. Kids gave him hell. Knew a woman once called Honor Kermode.

CHRISTINE: You can sit there all night, but I won't be there . . .

EDDIE: Where y'goin' then, kid? Club in town?

MARIE: I'm not goin' out . . . not in my condition . . .

(EDDIE *looks at her, hesitates, comes around to face her.*)

CHRISTINE: The state you're in, there'd be no point.

EDDIE: What condition, Marie?

MARIE: *I'm* havin' a baby; I am, I'm expectin'. (*Puts her hands across her stomach.*) And I want my make-up.

CHRISTINE: Nothin' can possibly come of it, y'wastin' your time even tryin'. (*She puts the phone down.*)

MARIE: Burnt orange . . .

BEN: Won't live long. Not in that state.

MARIE: It's under my bed.

BEN: I was found under a gooseberry bush . . . an' left on a bus . . .

MARIE: I left my make-up bag on a bus once . . . went t'Lost Property an' claimed an umbrella 'cos it was rainin' . . . but it's under my bed now where Babs an' the others can't find it.

EDDIE: Marie . . .

(*No answer.*)

Marie.

BEN: My wife used t'buy her make-up in bulk an' put it on with a trowel. The more lines there were, the more she plastered herself. Looked like our ceilin' in the end.

EDDIE: Marie, love.

BEN: Just before she died I bought her a cement mixer.

MARIE: Yes?

(CHRISTINE *comes out of the nurses' room, stands by the doorway.*)

EDDIE: Remember our little talk before, when you weren't so well . . . y'know . . .

MARIE: Marie cried, but Marie better now.

EDDIE: Yes I know, a lot better, good girl, but Marie, if you have another baby, you might be ill again . . . very very sick. Best not t'think about it hey? Forget all about it. Eddie go and get you some lipstick, dress you up all nice and glamorous, take you in to watch the television, see what programme's on, shall we?

BEN: *Watch with Mother.* (*Mouth tight shut as soon as he has said it.*)

(EDDIE *looks at him angrily but* MARIE *is delighted.*)

MARIE: Might be!

EDDIE: Y'just can't help yourself, can you, Ben? Tied down you'd still pipe up. (*Turns away, sees* CHRISTINE.)

BEN: I want a paper to read.

EDDIE: I'll get you one now.

CHRISTINE: There's one in here.

(*She goes into the nurses' room. An old* Liverpool Echo *lying on a chair.* EDDIE *follows her in.* MARIE *quietly puts a cushion off one of the chairs up her skirt. Sits down.*)

EDDIE: Marie thinks she's . . .

CHRISTINE: I know, I heard you talking to her. Poor sad bitch.

EDDIE: What about him, Jimmy.

CHRISTINE: Goin' down the Legion.

EDDIE: Got his priorities right at least.

CHRISTINE: Expectin' me to be at home waitin' for him when he gets back. Or else.

EDDIE: Or else what?

CHRISTINE: He'll come lookin' for us. Wherever we are.

EDDIE: I thought I'd get brought into it somewhere along the line.

CHRISTINE: I told him it wasn't anythin' t'do with you or anyone else.

EDDIE: Ahh, in that case I can rest easy in my bed tonight. (*Grabs hold of himself by the lapels of his coat as if being gripped by someone.*) Now, look Jimmy, old buddy, old pal, I've got definite assurances from your wife that I am not havin' it off with her, d'you appreci— Smack butt wallop! (*Holds his face.*)

CHRISTINE: You don't have to do anythin', y'know. I'm not askin' for anything of anyone, just to be . . . (*Aware that she is going to repeat Vera's earlier statement*) . . . on my . . . left alone.

EDDIE: (*Puts his arm around her.*) I vant to be alone.

(*She turns away.*)

CHRISTINE: I'm not one of your patients. (*Breaks free. Takes the paper and goes out.*)

EDDIE: Christine . . .

(CHRISTINE *goes into the lounge, gives the paper to* BEN. *Turns away.*)

BEN: (*Looking at the headlines*) This paper's three weeks old.

CHRISTINE: (*Harshly*) What d'you want me to do – bury it?

BEN: Jokes as well – an' all on the National Health.

EDDIE: (*As* CHRISTINE *comes back*) I'm going to get Marie made up and have a look in Montgomery. Why don't you just go ho—

CHRISTINE: Home?

EDDIE: Away from here. I'll give you the key to my flat; cover for you. Say you were sick.

CHRISTINE: Running away again, hey Eddie?

EDDIE: F'God's sake, woman, all I want you to do is get away from this – from the phone – from them – for a while.

CHRISTINE: But the state they're in . . .

EDDIE: The state we're all in . . . All right, don't go, stay, but just go over to the other lounge, sit down, have a smoke, make everyone some tea or something. Let this lot rip themselves t'bits for ten minutes if that's what they want t'do. Y'can't be everywhere all the time, love. We've got twenty-two patients between us tonight, plus the threat of a madman outside the walls t'cater for – an' apart from sedatin' the buggers, I haven't seen more than about five of them.

CHRISTINE: I won't be long.

EDDIE: That's all I want. I'll just go and get Marie's make-up case and then I'll . . . sort Vera out.

(CHRISTINE *looks at him.*)

Yes, I will be nice. (*Turns away.*) Even though I still don't believe her.

(EDDIE *looks across the lounge towards* MARIE *with her hands folded across her stomach.* BEN *reading the paper.* PETE *for once does not notice him as he goes.* CHRISTINE *stands briefly and then follows him.* BEN *is already talking to* MARIE.)

BEN: Got any stumps?

MARIE: Got none.

BEN: (*To* PETE) Got any stumps?

PETE: You killed my goldfish.

BEN: Better off dead than trapped in there, bouncin' off the glass, gettin' stared at all day long.

PETE: It was my friend.

BEN: Give us 10p then.

PETE: No.

BEN: (*To* MARIE) Give us 10p.

MARIE: Shan't.

BEN: Go on.

MARIE: Don't want to.

BEN: It's for me daughter Louise, go on, give us 10p, y'like me phonin' me daughters, don't y'?

MARIE: I haven't got 10p.

BEN: (*To* PETE) Give us 10p an' I'll tell y' who really killed y' goldfish.

PETE: I need it more than you, I'm goin' places.

BEN: You're not goin' nowhere, an' you know it. (*Looks at them.*) Bugger y' then. I'll use me own money!

(BEN *stands, giggles, takes 10p out of his pocket, goes over to the phone, as the other two watch happily, dials a number, waits for it to ring, the pips go, he puts the money in.*)

Is that you, Louise – well, fuck off then! (*He slams the phone down. Exulted. Comes back to the others.* MARIE *has obviously liked it.* PETE *stops painting for the moment.* BEN *sits down, well satisfied.*)

Best value for 10p in the whole world.

MARIE: Lend us 10p.

BEN: Use your own money, I know where y'hide yours.

MARIE: Lend us 10p, Petie, go on, an' I won't hit you.

PETE: Y'll still hit me, y'always do.

MARIE: You're dead t'morrow, you are, just you wait.

PETE: Won't be here tomorrow.

(MARIE *gets a small purse out of the pocket of her teddy's dress, takes out 10p, goes to the phone, looks at the wall where numbers are scrawled. Dials a number.*)

MARIE: Is that Mr R. Soles, well fu— (*Holds the phone away from herself, shocked. Puts it back quickly on the hook.*) He told *me* t'fuck off!

PETE: I want a go! (*Stands up. Nervous and excited*) I have got 10p, I want a go!

(*Goes over to the phone,* MARIE *still standing there.*)

It's my go.

(*She moves slightly away from the phone.* PETE *gets hold of the receiver. Stops. Looks around at the others.*)

I've . . . I've got no one to phone up. (*Takes his hand away from the phone.*)

MARIE: I know who you can phone up, Petie . . . my friends. You can phone my friends up.

PETE: You haven't got no friends, neither.

MARIE: Yes I have, these're my friends, they like me . . .

PETE: You phone them up an' I'll speak to them.

MARIE: Give us y' 10p.

(*He moves away from her, wrapping the telephone flex around himself as he goes.*)

PETE: No, you'll take it an' not give it me back an' I'll not get a go at the phone. I'll put it in, you dial the numbers.

MARIE: All right then. (*She starts dialling the numbers. Her cushion slips halfway down, and she pushes it back up.*)

PETE: What're your friends' names?

MARIE: One of them's called Bobby – he'll answer the phone.

(PETE *has the telephone flex wrapped slackly around his neck as he puts his 10p by the slot, the pips go,* MARIE *pushes his hand and he puts the money in. She waits briefly to hear a voice, then hands him the phone.*)

PETE: (*Racing*) Is that you, Bobby, is it hey, well fuck off! Then! (*Looks around at the others with pride, the phone still in his hand. Turns to terror as someone speaks at the other end of the phone.*) Ea . . . Ea . . . Eaton Road P . . . Police Station . . . Y've made me ph— phone the police, y've made me say . . .

(*He throws the phone down. But every time he throws the phone down and tries to move away, the flex drags him back and the phone jumps off the hook, making him even more manic.* MARIE *and* BEN *laugh at him. He panics. High-pitched yelp.*)

Mmmmmm . . .

(*The others laugh at him. Finally he releases himself.*)

PETE: They'll catch me now, they will, I'm trapped, I'm trapped in here. Mnnnnn . . .

(*The phone rings in the nurses' room as* PETE *backs towards it. He is close to it. Loud.* PETE *butts the ceiling, so to speak.*)

MARIE: Phone's ringing.

BEN: It'll be f'you, Pete.

PETE: I'll tell them, I will, I'll tell them who it was, I don't care. (*Moves towards the phone in the nurses' room.*) Nnnnn . . . (*He gets to the door, edges towards the phone, then rushes at it. Grabs it, picks it up and speaks all in one motion.*) Mmmmmm, I never said fuck off it wasn't me and anyway they made me do it! (*Slams the phone down, rushes out of the nurses' room, goes back.*) I told them, did y'hear me, I told them who it was. (*Sits down.*) They won't take me away. (*Begins painting.*)

(MARIE *sits back, holding her lump.* BEN *picks up the paper.*)

BEN: (*Reading from the paper*) Man. United thrashed again! 4–0! (*Giggles.*) Atkinson's Army bite the dust. (*Pauses, glances a* MARIE.) Not a patch on the team in the fifties. Y'd have liked that team, Marie, Busby's babes.

MARIE: Babes in the Wood!

BEN: (*Disappointed*) Is that all?

MARIE: It's a nice story.

BEN: Huh nice . . . (*Looks at his paper.*) 'Ladies!'

MARIE: And gentlemen . . .

BEN: The first ever national newspaper f'women . . . produced by the National Housewives Association . . . this week's free offer, twin sachets of bromide and arsenic . . . what a waste of paper . . . Important issues like why do we have to spend our lives dancing backwards . . . If I let him, will he respect me . . . Now I've let him, where's he gone? . . . Is it enough to marry for love?

MARIE: Marry . . . (*Calls out*) Marie, love, y'tea's ready.

BEN: (*Giggles as he looks at the paper.*) 'Are you retired early? Are you an expert bacon cutter? If you are, G. A. Peacock of London Road would like to hear from you . . .' (*Rips the advert out.*) Keep that, might come in handy.

MARIE: Andy. Handy Pandy, Handy Pandy, puddin' an' pie, kissed the girls and made them cry . . .

(*As she sings,* EDDIE *comes back with her make-up case, puts it on her lap, pats her head, carries on through the lounge, going out the opposite doors. As soon as he goes,* BEN, *who has been following his flight plan, starts again.*)

BEN: Here we are, the best bit of the paper, 'Births, Deaths and the Destruction of Manhood.' Not many births, lots of bloody deaths . . . family plannin' . . . didn't need it when . . . when I had a family.

MARIE: Family. Fa-mi-ly. (*She is applying the lipstick to herself and continues to pile it on as the scene progresses until she gets upset.*) Marie an'. . . ?

BEN: The she-wolf had her own answer t'that problem . . . an Aspro between her knees . . . that was the pill in our day . . . used t'go to bed as if it was a disaster area. (*He looks down at the paper.*)

MARIE: (*Holds herself tightly, cries out sharply*) Oh!

BEN: Kickin' is it?

MARIE: I remember. It was the school whatsits . . .

BEN: (*Glances at her, reads again*) Williams, March the 23rd, 1986, at Mill Road Maternity Hospital, to Patricia and Alex, a son, Paul John, many thanks to the nursing staff for a safe delivery . . . (*He looks back at her for her reaction.*)

MARIE: No . . . no, not deliver . . . not deliver . . . taken away. My . . . my . . . my baby . . . boy.

BEN: 'Though my eyes may not always be weeping, and my heart's not always sad, there is never a moment passes that I don't long for the baby boy I once had . . .'

MARIE: Yes. (*Smiles contented, then another memory.*) *No!*

BEN: Every one a loving memory at twenty pence a word . . .

MARIE: (*Alert, bolt upright*) I remember. I was very young. They locked me away for bein' young. An' havin' a baby . . .

BEN: Nothin' but sweet words . . . happy days . . . lifetime of kindness . . . no one ever suffered shite, no one ever destroyed anyone or hurt each other in the Death columns of the *Liverpool Echo* . . . (*Looks down again at the paper. He is now totally lost in himself.*) . . . Jacobs . . . there's a Jacobs . . . 'Dad's smiling eyes are sleeping, a golden heart at rest, God only broke our hearts to prove to us He only takes the best . . . Broken-hearted Brenda.' (*Again a nervous giggle.*)

Miserable Maureen, Destroyed Debra . . .

MARIE: They can't take this baby away like they . . . (*Fades. She clutches her stomach.*)

BEN: (*Looks up from the paper, stares out.*) 'One thing you could say about my Dad, Ben, He was a bastard amongst men.' Laughing Louise and Happy Harriet . . . (*Lets the paper drop between his knees. Puts his head down.*)

MARIE: . . . Like the last time . . . (*Again another memory breaks upon her, another flashback and she holds herself tightly.*) Ben! Ben!

(*His chair is not within touching distance but she puts her free hand out. He has lost all interest in putting the knife into her. Does not look up. She turns towards* PETE. *She stands, holding on to her 'baby'/cushion.* PETE *looks at her, and then straight down again.*)

Petie! I know what happened to him. They took him away . . . but I know what happened . . . *PETIE!*

PETE: (*Head down*) I'm goin', t'night. T'night's the night. Sod me dad.

MARIE: I know what happened to him. I do.

PETE: I know an' all. I even saw him. He came back to Sheffield all right. A woman in every port includin' Sheffield . . . stood at the bus stop in a pork pie hat . . . linkin' a woman . . . what weren't my mam . . . got on the Chesterfield bus . . . and went away . . .

MARIE: No, that wasn't what happened to him.

(BEN *stands,* MARIE *sits down, no longer erect, slouched.*)

BEN: (*To nobody, already fumbling in his pocket*) Give us 10p. (*Doesn't wait for an answer, goes straight over to telephone, dials a number rapidly, the pips go, he puts his money in, is almost incoherent.*) Is that you, is it Harriet? Well . . . (*He sobs.*) Well . . . (*He leaves the phone dangling, comes back a yard or so towards his chair.*) She came out the wrong way round, Harriet did, an' pissed in the doctor's face. (*Laughs, chokes on it.*) So my wife always told everyone we ever met. Never could believe a word she told me though. Told me many a time she . . . she . . . loved

. . . me. (*Snorts.*) Two of a kind we were 'In loveless memory of my unbeloved wife Pat, all through our miserable marriage you were one miserable twat.' (*To the phone*) Harriet? (*Screams*) Harriet!! Gone. (*He puts the phone back on the hook.*) But not forgiven . . . And no more ten pences . . . (*Sits down and looks at the others, stands again.*) 'Here I stand, your slave. A poor infirm weak and despised old man . . . and to deal plainly, I fear I am not in my perfect mind.' (*He sits down.*)

MARIE: (*Pause.*) Wha'?

BEN: King Lear.

MARIE: That's a funny name, is he a wrestler?

(*No answer from* BEN.)

'King Lear Webster.' Nah . . .

(CHRISTINE *comes back in through the doors by the nurses' room. Walks into the lounge. There doesn't seem to have been any change, apart from* MARIE'*s lipstick.*)

CHRISTINE: Finished with the paper, Ben? (*She picks it up, folds it, walks away.*)

BEN: (*Lets her go.*) No, I haven't.

(CHRISTINE *walks back, goes to give it back to him.*)

Sorry, I've changed my mind, I have finished with it.

MARIE: I want it, I want it. (*Snatches it.*) I want to read the names.

CHRISTINE: I've got a better idea, Marie, why don't we all go down to the other lounge and watch the television?

MARIE: I want to read the names.

CHRISTINE: You get lots of names on the television, Marie. At the end of the programme they give you whole lists of them.

MARIE: Y'never get a chance t'read them, they go too fast. (*Finds the page, begins to look at them.*)

BEN: Who wants t'be called 'Granada' anyway?

CHRISTINE: Well, come on, Ben, how about you? I've made some tea and coffee down there. Might even find you a ciggie.

BEN: I'm not goin' down there, I'm not watchin' television –

y'never know what you're going to see next – Soddin' Selina Scott, Esther Rantzen and her friggin' teeth, fuckin' Jan Leeming . . . Margaret Thatcher the female führer, friend of the poor. (*Laughs.*) Friend of the poor.

CHRISTINE: Right, Peter, how about you, been painting all day y'know. I'm sure you could do with a rest.

PETE: This is important, this is. Got to be done tonight.

CHRISTINE: As I was going out of the lounge before, I could have sworn I heard the announcer mention something about a travel programme on Hawaii.

PETE: (*Looks up at her, then back to his painting.*) I know all there is to know already.

(CHRISTINE *looks at them, looks again at her watch.*)

CHRISTINE: It's time for bed soon, you know, but if you go down to the other lounge, I might arrange with the night staff for you to stay up a bit later.

(*No interest whatsoever.*)

BEN: (*After a pause.*) If I can have a bottle of Mackies, I'll go.

CHRISTINE: The off-licence'll be shut, Ben.

BEN: Stayin' here then. (*Looks up at her.*) I want to stay here anyway, somethin's happenin' here, isn't it? Somethin' good's goin' to happen, isn't it? There's goin' to be trouble here all right, I'm not soft . . . all those phone calls. I know.

CHRISTINE: Oh come on, Ben . . .

BEN: I'm goin' to stay here all night an' wait.

CHRISTINE: (*Goes down to her haunches, near to him.*) Ben . . .

(*He stares straight ahead.*)

Ben, you've been threatened enough today, one way or another, and I don't want to threaten you any more, but if you don't do as you're told . . .

BEN: Who d'you think you are? My mother? (*Giggles, peers at her.*) Y'might be.

(*The phone rings again. Again loudly.*)

PETE: It wasn't me, it wasn't me, I didn't do it. (*He stands up quickly, looks towards the nurses' room.*)

MARIE: Phone's ringing.

PETE: They made me do it. I've already told them. They made me say dirty words to a policeman. Only I didn't know it was a policeman . . .

(CHRISTINE *stands by* BEN'*s chair as the phone continues to ring.* PETE *backs away.* EDDIE *walks through the doors opposite to the nurses' room.* VERA *is with him. He is near to carrying her. One arm on her shoulder, the other underneath her arm supporting her. She looks dazed, a classic victim of shock.* EDDIE *gives her his every attention – totally different from his earlier approach to her.* PETE *is overjoyed at seeing him. As soon as* EDDIE *enters he points at the nurses' room where the phone is ringing.*)

EDDIE: The phone, Christine, come on.

(CHRISTINE *goes to the phone. Picks it up and drops it down.*)

PETE: (*As* CHRISTINE *goes*) Barry . . . Barry . . . (*Goes over to him.*) It's them, Barry, it's them, they're closin' in, they know I'm here . . .

(*The phone stops.* CHRISTINE *returns.*)

EDDIE: Back to y'paintin' old son, y'get yourself too excited for your own good . . . no one'll get you here, now just sit down will y'.

PETE: But . . .

EDDIE: Can't y'see I'm busy.

BEN: (*As* VERA *passses them, sings quietly the television advert for Danish bacon*) 'Danish bacon, bacon, bacon . . .'

(CHRISTINE *hits out at him, smacks him hard across the face.*)

You little bitch . . .

MARIE: Baybee, baybee . . .

(*She stands, follows* VERA *and* EDDIE, *compares stomachs, pushes the cushion into position, notes how she walks bowlegged.* PETE *comes over to* EDDIE, *takes hold of his sleeve, gently at first.* EDDIE *sits* VERA *down.* MARIE *sits in the nearest chair and adopts her manner. As this happens the phone rings again.* CHRISTINE *shouts out in despair. Runs to the phone, grabs hold of it.*)

CHRISTINE: (*Cold*) Will you please get off the phone, I am very busy . . . I'm putting the phone down, Jimmy . . . (*As he speaks, she becomes alarmed.*) No . . . listen Jimmy, don't come here, don't . . . *JIMMY!*

(*She holds the phone away from herself and then throws it down. Sits slumped over the phone.*)

PETE: (*Still tugging*) Barry . . .

EDDIE: Now listen, Vera, y'sitting down, right?

PETE: *Barry* . . .

(CHRISTINE *rises, moves into the lounge.*)

EDDIE: I don't want you to move, understand, not just yet, I'm going to . . .

PETE: Barry, listen Barry . . .

EDDIE: (*Pulling his sleeve away*) I'm going to get you some medicine and then Nurse Matthews'll take you to bed because you need some sleep very badly, don't you?

(*The phone rings again. Everyone seems to jump.*)

PETE: Barry, it's them, Barry, it's them!

EDDIE: (*Turns on* PETE) *Sit down!* (*To* CHRISTINE) Answer the sodding phone and then leave it off the hook, bugger them.

(CHRISTINE *goes to the phone again.* PETE *stays where he is. Bewildered.*)

PETE: (*Desperately*) But, Barry . . .

EDDIE: (*Quietly trying to control himself*) Sit down, Peter. (*Still quietly but with more emphasis*) *Sit down.*

(PETE *stays stubbornly where he is. He has hold of* EDDIE's *sleeve throughout.* CHRISTINE *lifts the phone up.* JIMMY *is breathing heavily down it.*)

CHRISTINE: (*After her immediate revulsion*) What's the matter, Jimmy, have you got asthma?

(*She goes to put the phone down then leaves it off the hook on the desk. As* CHRISTINE *does this,* VERA *begins her story.*)

VERA: (*Distant, no feeling apparent in her words*) I couldn't run far. I walked home, walked . . . my back hurt. I left my money here in my coat pocket. And my ciggies. Through the new estate. Across the . . .

(CHRISTINE *comes into the lounge. Towards* VERA . . .)

EDDIE: Yes, fine, all right Vera, it's all right, you don't have to . . .

VERA: Across the wasteland . . . in the dark . . .

PETE: Barry . . .

VERA: . . . down our path . . . past the broken gate . . . the lights were on . . . I put my hand through the letterbox . . . (*Mimes limply with her hand, lets it fall again.*) . . . and took the key out . . . on a string.

EDDIE: Shush now, shush . . .

CHRISTINE: That's enough, Vera . . .

VERA: Smell of stale nappies . . . (*Laughs.*) . . . the Drifters on the record player . . . his coat on the banisters . . . front room door not quite shut . . . I stood there . . .

EDDIE: Yes, love, I'm sure you did, now . . .

VERA: And there they were on the couch . . . doing it . . .

(EDDIE *reaches out, puts his hands at either side of her face.*)

EDDIE: No, no, Vera, stop . . .

VERA: Her knickers were over the fireguard . . .

MARIE: Lady wee-weed . . .

EDDIE: (*Turning, quietly*) Christine.

VERA: And then I screamed. And screamed. And screamed.

(*She screams.* MARIE *screams.*)

PETE: (*Again at* EDDIE*'s elbow*) I'm goin' now, Barry, right now, before they come.

EDDIE: (*To* CHRISTINE) 100 milligrams largactil, intramuscular, *quickly*.

(CHRISTINE *turns towards the nurses' room.* EDDIE *tries to comfort* VERA. PETE *holds on to him.* EDDIE *pushes* PETE *away.* CHRISTINE *takes the equipment from the cupboard.*)

PETE: But they'll be here soon . . .

EDDIE: (*As* PETE *paws at him*) Stop it, Peter.

PETE: But I've got to have help, I'm goin' now . . .

EDDIE: Peter! (PETE *has his arms around him from the back.*) Get your arms off me!

VERA: She had her legs up in the air.

PETE: Hawaii bound, that's me, that's where I'm goin', on a schooner out of Liv . . .

EDDIE: (*Pulling himself away from* PETE, *turning on him, as* CHRISTINE *comes back*) You little schizo, you aren't going to Hawaii, you're going nowhere, I am not Barry Vincent, I am not six foot one, fourteen stone, with black curly hair, flat feet an' a birthmark on my chest. I do not screw all the women in C. F. Mott. Can't you see, you dumb daft soft bastard, don't you know they stopped looking for you when they found you thirteen years ago, can't you live with reality for more than ten seconds of your tiny life?

(CHRISTINE *pulls him away from* PETE *and he turns his back*.)

I'm sorry, Peter.

CHRISTINE: Eddie.

PETE: (*Formally, with great dignity, as if he was swearing an oath*) I know you are not Barry Vincent, I know I am not going to Hawaii, I know my dad wears a pork pie hat an' my mam is dead. I know all of that, you don't have to tell me. (*He turns and goes back to his painting, but sits on the floor*.)

EDDIE: Peter . . .

(CHRISTINE *gives him the hypodermic needle and he reluctantly turns back to* VERA *who is still sitting trance-like after her scream*.)

I'm not even sure if this is right, the state she's in, she could go either way. Come on Vera, darlin', let's see what sort of arms you've got . . . my, look at those lovely blue lines . . . now then, who's going to have a bonny . . . (*Realizes what he is about to say . . . the wrong thing*.)

MARIE: Me!

EDDIE: . . . old sleep then?

MARIE: Oh.

EDDIE: Won't be long now, half an hour an' all y'troubles 'll be over, one nice long sleep coming up . . . there we go, didn't feel a thing, did you?

(*He has slipped the needle in as* CHRISTINE *holds her arm and he talks to her.* VERA *does not appear even to notice the needle.* EDDIE *picks up the apparatus, takes it back to the nurses' room.* CHRISTINE *goes over to* VERA *and* MARIE, *lights a cigarette for each of them, goes to light one for herself, sees* BEN *looking at her, gives it to him.* PETE *is folding the map of the world up.* MARIE *has edged her chair over so that she is sitting next to* VERA. *She is copying everything that she does – which isn't much.* BEN *is screwed up in his chair, feet up, arms around himself, eyes staring out, and occasionally mouthing words that cannot be heard.*)

Finished with that then, have you, old son?

PETE: (*Ignoring* EDDIE) I shook hands with Barry at the door. He said, 'Are y' goin' now, Pete?' an' I said 'Yes I am', an' he said 'Well good luck lad, send us a postcard when y' get there' an' he put his arm around me an' I walked away, an' then he shouted to me as I got t'the lift an' I hurried back an' he said, 'How far would you be now if I hadn't called y' back?'

EDDIE: Aye, that sounds like Barry.

PETE: I got a lift from Prescot to the motorway an' started walkin', lookin' for the turn off t'Sheffield, but I never did find it. Got chased off the motorway an' all after a bit; mist comin' down, it were beginnin' t'snow as well, an' I started takin' me clothes off, wrappin' them up under me arm, found another road, people shouted an' waved at me from their cars, an' an old woman got out of a Morris Minor an' came for me with her umbrella; got t'this big house at the start of some village, knocked on the door in me knacker; were opened up by a vicar an' his housekeeper holdin' lanterns, like Frankenstein's Castle. I ran off across their lawn an' they chased after me. I were buggered an' they brought me down in a bed of dead chrysanths. They both had bad breath. By this time I'd been seen by so many people all the loony bins in two counties were after me. Almost ripped apart I were by two sets of ambulance drivers, one from Yorkshire an' the other from Lancashire – both of them fightin' over me. I didn't care who won, but what happened was Lancashire got me an' Yorkshire got me clothes.

EDDIE: Long time ago, that was, Pete.

PETE: (*Pause.*) I know.

EDDIE: Bad things happen t'most people some time or other, Peter, fact of life, an' for a few of them it's the end of the road, but y'know, an awful lot of people manage to get over it eventually, or at least learn t'live with it. I mean . . . (*Hesitates, glances at* CHRISTINE.) . . . there were things happened t'me when I was eighteen . . .

PETE: I . . . I was eighteen . . .

EDDIE: . . . When I was in . . . Malaya . . . (*As much for* CHRISTINE*'s information*) . . . two hundred of us stuck in the soddin' jungle till God knows when, right in the middle of the arsehole of the Empire – (*Laughs bitterly.*) – an' arsehole's the word . . . no women, no wives, no one-trick five pound whores, no one. And there's always some blokes somewhere who have to find somethin' . . . they found me. I was a very pretty boy, Peter. So they said . . . but . . . but y'know, y'try an' pick up the pieces . . .

CHRISTINE: But it's not the same f'Peter, it's different for him, y'can't expect . . .

EDDIE: What I'm saying is even if y'going to be sick all y'life, just a little bit sick, no harm to society, there should be a soddin' way y'can be sick in the outside world as well.

CHRISTINE: But you can't expect him to pick up the pieces – not after all this time.

EDDIE: I thought it was too late for me thirty-five years ago, Christine, but it wasn't, and it isn't now. *Is it*?

PETE: Me mam said me dad went funny as well, y'know after they got married. All that goin' away t'sea, that weren't me dad, that's what she said; said he got scared in the shallow end at the swimmin' baths. It were another man that went away t'sea. Two people my dad were . . .

EDDIE: An' he's been outside all his life, Peter.

(PETE *stands as he talks, takes hold of his drawing, shows it to* EDDIE. *It simply says* 'Hawaii or bust'.)

PETE: Y'right, an' I'm goin' tonight, Barry, tonight's the night. I really am. (*Walks towards the door by the nurses' room.*) I'm just off to fetch me things.

EDDIE: Course y'are. (*Watches him go.*) All to bed in ten minutes, d'you hear? Saturday tomorrow, out in the gardens, gettin' a tan for the summer. Bit of a bronzy.

BEN: She hit me.

EDDIE: Only 'cos she got to you before I did. I'd have cheerfully strangled you.

BEN: Wants t'pick on someone her own size. And sex.

EDDIE: Ten minutes, don't forget. An' I'm not going anywhere, I'm just here, so no tricks . . .

(EDDIE *turns and the second he starts moving away,* BEN *steals out of his chair and goes over to* VERA, *takes out his 'Bacon Slicer' advert and puts it in her hand. He cannot restrain a giggle, then suddenly stops, turns away. But* EDDIE *turns too and catches him.*)

Come here, Ben, *come here*!

(VERA *looks at the advert but with seemingly no reaction. Lets it drop to the floor.* BEN *looks back over his shoulder at her as he goes towards* EDDIE. *Stands at* EDDIE*'s side, looks sideways at him. Flinches.*)

You, you're not leavin' my sight. Stand there.

(*He places him outside the door of the nurses' room, leaning on the wall of the padded cell.*)

BEN: Goin' to give me the cane, are you? Put me in detention? Keep me in. (*Laughs.*) Keep me in!

EDDIE: (*To* CHRISTINE) What's happening?

CHRISTINE: I don't know.

EDDIE: What did he say?

CHRISTINE: Said he was comin'.

EDDIE: Oh Christ, will he?

CHRISTINE: I don't bloody well know – two minutes later he

was on again (*shudders*) the old heavy breathin'. Sounded like a sick goat. (*Pause.*) Shall we warn security to stop him?

EDDIE: They couldn't stop my grandmother, those two. One's got a limp an' the other one's blind. What about the police?

CHRISTINE: (*Laughs.*) Once they find out it's domestic they call 'Seconds out' an' bugger off. (*Pause.*) Vera all right?

EDDIE: (*Moves into the corridor, looks across at a very still* VERA.) Yes. (*Goes back in.*) Are *you* all right?

CHRISTINE: He was in a terrible state with himself, Jimmy.

EDDIE: Sod Jimmy. (*Goes over to her suitcases, brings them out.*) Here, I'll order a taxi, get you back to my place.

CHRISTINE: When he loses his temper there's no controllin' him.

EDDIE: So why be around – it'll be no discovery gettin' y'nose broken again.

(EDDIE *picks up the phone.*)

CHRISTINE: No, I'm not runnin' away from him. I'd only run in a circle an' come back. Y've seen them in here, battered wives, they always go back. Like a magnet at the end of their feller's fist.

EDDIE: But it's not going to happen to you.

CHRISTINE: (*Quietly*) Going to look after me, are you, Eddie?

EDDIE: Stop it! (*Puts the phone down.*)

CHRISTINE: Like Vera, now that she's in need of lookin' after.

EDDIE: It's not the same.

CHRISTINE: You want them to be sick, don't you? No danger t'you then, are they?

EDDIE: What a bitch of a thing t'say. Now of all times.

CHRISTINE: That's why you came here in the first place, wasn't it?

EDDIE: I was invalided out of the Army – I couldn't get another –

CHRISTINE: For yourself, nobody else. Just like me, your own life in a mess . . .

EDDIE: What're you doin' t'me?

CHRISTINE: A peacetime prisoner of war, just as institutionalized as all these . . . prisoners of war.

EDDIE: Christine!

BEN: (*Outside the door*) I'd twat her one, I would. No messin'. That's how they start y'know, pickin' at y'flesh . . .

EDDIE: Get out – go on, get out. (*Goes angrily towards the door.*)

(BEN *scuttles back into the lounge. Heads straight for and sits by* VERA *and* MARIE.)

CHRISTINE: No wonder y'good with the hopeless cases, Eddie.

EDDIE: What is this – some of your own back? Who can *I* hurt? Is that what it is?

CHRISTINE: All y'best mates are nutters. No drinkin' mates, old friends, girl friends . . . or any other kind of friend.

EDDIE: (*Defensively*) I was never that much bothered. Never been one f'much company.

CHRISTINE: Not since Malaya, hey?
Had a bit too much company then, didn't you?

EDDIE: (*Laughs nervously.*) You bitch. I think Ben might be right after all.

CHRISTINE: I'm not comin' back with you, Eddie, that's what I'm tryin' to say.

EDDIE: Y'could have thought of easier ways of tellin' me, instead of some second-rate psychoanalysis an' bringing up my war wounds.

CHRISTINE: *You* brought them up.

EDDIE: Oh boy am I havin' fun tonight. First of all you break me up verbally, an' any time now . . .

CHRISTINE: Why don't *you* go home? I'll ring for a taxi . . .

EDDIE: What's come over you?

CHRISTINE: Remember what I said before about closin' the door f'the last time an' not feelin' any different? Well, I was wrong; I feel it now. I've escaped, I've got out of my institution.

EDDIE: And none of us have? Or ever will? (*Pause.*)

CHRISTINE: (*Moves towards the door.*) I'm going over to put the television room to bed.

EDDIE: (*Flatly*) Some mattress that'll have to be.

(*She goes to the door.* EDDIE *sits down.*)

BEN: (*As* CHRISTINE *leaves*) Bully!

(*They have all nearly finished their cigarettes.* MARIE *only smoking hers when* VERA *does.* BEN *stubs his out and puts his stump in his top pocket.*)

Bad for y', y'know, smokin' when y'having a baby. Did y'know that? Not seen the adverts? Know what they say, don't y', Marie – could lose your baby if y' smoke durin' y'pregnancy.

(MARIE *has just inhaled. Gushes the smoke out, looks at* VERA *who is still smoking, doesn't know what to do.*)

Wouldn't like that to happen again, would y'? Not after the last time.

(MARIE *stubs her cigarette out, looks at* VERA, *grabs her cigarette and stubs that out too.* VERA *stares at her with no expression.*)

MARIE: It's bad for y' – y'might lose y'baby.

(VERA *laughs wildly,* MARIE *puzzled but after a second laughs too in a similar fashion.* VERA *holds her stomach.*)

VERA: Ooooh, y'little sod.

MARIE: Ooooh, yeah, y'little sod.

BEN: What did happen, the last time? Hey, Marie? Y'can tell me.

MARIE: Can't. Won't.

BEN: Give y'another ciggie.

MARIE: (*Eyes light up for a second.*) No! Not tellin'. (*In the same breath*) It was the schools attendance. He did it.

BEN: Did more than knock on your door hey, Marie?

MARIE: Always there. Even when I was at school, he'd come.

BEN: On the off chance of an unexpected holy day.

MARIE: Me mam didn't want me at home any more, but he got . . . put away an' all.

BEN: But you were havin' his baby, weren't you? Carryin' it around for him, free of charge, bein' sick every mornin', getting bigger every day, y' feet disappearin' from y'vision, dresses not fittin' y' . . .

MARIE: They examined me. One day they ex . . . (*Fades away.*)

BEN: And then what did they do, Marie. What did they do then?

MARIE: (*Struggling*) They . . . they . . . spoke to me.
(VERA *is looking at her, but there is still no expression on her face.*)
That was all, they spoke to me.

BEN: And you lost your baby?

MARIE: Not tellin'.

BEN: Just like that? It must have been a cutting speech.

MARIE: They told me . . . what they were goin' to do.

VERA: It's nothin' to what I'm goin' to do.

BEN: (*Immediately to her*) What're you goin' to do then hey? (*No answer.*)

MARIE: They were nice to me. They said it wouldn't hurt. It didn't hurt, Ben. Not then.

BEN: (*Still to* VERA) Get your own back. I would. Even a woman's allowed that.

MARIE: When I woke up, me baby was gone. They took my baby away. Then it hurt.

BEN: (*At* VERA) Do somethin' they'll never forget, somethin' that'll live along with them every day of their lives. Do more than leave it on a bus, take more revenge than that.

MARIE: (*To herself*) And I know where they put it an' all. Nurse told me. Nurse Lister. 'Cos I was a naughty girl. She shouted at me. Sang 'Rock-A-Bye Baby' to me an' laughed. Said, 'We took him out t'the lavatory an' put the lid on him.' (*She is crying.*) I went down there after but it was gone. She followed me in there, she wasn't a very nice person, she stood laughing at the doorway as I looked for my baby. 'You won't find him now,' she said, 'he's not there now.' An' she took hold of my arm an' led me to the incinerator where they burnt all the rubbish an' the things they didn't want an' she left me holdin' the little . . . door.

(VERA *stands, laughs hysterically.* MARIE *attempts to copy her but halfway through, she cries.* PETE *comes back in through the entrance by the nurses' room.* VERA *walks over towards that entrance, followed by* MARIE.)

BEN: Don't forget now!

(PETE *is carrying a plastic carrier bag full of clothes, and his Hawaii sign. He is wearing a pork pie hat.*)

PETE: I'm goin' now, I've just come t'say goodbye. (*Looks at* VERA.) It's been nice knowin' you.

(*She walks straight past him.*)

I hope y'get better soon.

(MARIE *walks past him.*)

Bye, Marie, I'm goin' now . . . er wha' y'crying for, Marie?

MARIE: They're not goin' to take this one away from me.

(VERA *goes past the nurses' room.* EDDIE *looks up, comes to the door.*)

EDDIE: Where y'goin', Vera?

(*She looks vacantly at him. She carries on walking to the door.*)

Vera . . .

VERA: I'm goin' to the lavatory.

MARIE: Y'won't find it now, it's too late . . .

(*She stops following* VERA. EDDIE *takes hold of her.*)

EDDIE: You stay here, Marie, I'll . . . (*Looks towards the door where* VERA *has gone.*)

PETE: I'm goin' now, Barry, headin' down the road, moon's up, I've just looked through the window . . . stars are out . . .

EDDIE: (*Guides* MARIE *back, sits her in a chair away from* BEN.) Lovely night for it then . . .

PETE: I've got the map . . . (*Taps his pocket.*)

EDDIE: Right then.

PETE: I wouldn't have gone if it'd been rainin'; all the lines would have run on me sign . . . but er, it's not rainin'. Is it?

EDDIE: No, it's not.

PETE: So . . . I'll be goin' then.

(Phone rings loudly. PETE *jumps. So does* EDDIE.)

I'll just wait for the phone call. Might be f'me. Might be the police.

(EDDIE *stays still.*)

Y'd better answer it. Can't go if it's them. Be out lookin' for me.

(EDDIE *moves towards the phone.*)

Wouldn't be safe. They'd be searchin' for me. Not safe at all. Have to lie low. For a couple of days. Week or so. Maybe more . . .

EDDIE: *(In the nurses' room, picks the phone up.)* Yes? Oh, Dave . . . lookin' f'Christine . . . y'didn't, did y'? . . . No, no, my fault, listen call the police, right away . . . no it won't be domestic, not when he hits me. *(Puts the phone down. He is obviously very scared.)*

PETE: *(Still in the lounge)* Was it them? Was it?

(No answer. EDDIE *takes off his white coat, pulls out his shirt front, takes his jacket off a hook, stands his hair up, walks out of the doorway, goes to the padded cell, unlocks it, leaves the door open a mere couple of inches.)*

PETE: Was it the police?

EDDIE: What? Oh no, no, you're safe, Peter.

PETE: Oh. Well. Er still, it could have been a trick, y'know. Yeah, might have been them. Y'never kn— *(Notices the state of* EDDIE *for the first time.)* What y'dressed like that for, Eddie?

EDDIE: Barry. I'm Barry Vincent. Remember?

PETE: What y'dressed like that for, Barry?

EDDIE: It's . . . hot in here! Like Hawaii, Pete.

PETE: An' y'shirt's hanging' out.

EDDIE: *(Looking at the far doorway)* Latest fashion, Pete.

(Starts to move across to BEN *and* MARIE.)

PETE: An' y'hair's stickin' up.

EDDIE: All right, Pete, now just don't forget who I am, hey?

PETE: No . . . I won't.

EDDIE: Come on you two, off to bed. (*To* MARIE) 'Up the stairs and say your prayers, you'd better be good children.' (*Lifts her hurriedly as he sings.*) There you go, Marie. Hurry up, Ben.

MARIE: (*Looking at* EDDIE) Have y'wet yourself, Eddie?

EDDIE: No, course I haven't, but let's take you down for a wee-wee, hey? Y'can get Vera out of there for me, there's a good girl.

MARIE: (*As* EDDIE *pushes her and tries to get hold of* BEN) She's lookin' for my baby, but she won't find it . . .

EDDIE: The state of your face. Y'mascara's all over the place, have to wash it all . . .

(*The far doors burst open and* JIMMY *appears. Dishevelled, out of breath, wide-eyed, the worse for drink.* BEN *jumps, thinking it is Vera's husband:* EDDIE *slumps, lets go of* MARIE *who plops back into her chair.* PETE *takes two steps rapidly backwards and then comes forward again.* JIMMY *goes over to* BEN.)

JIMMY: Where is she?

BEN: She's in the toilets, I didn't tell her to do anythin', it wasn't me.

JIMMY: (*Picks* BEN *up by the lapels of his jacket.*) Christine Matthews, she's a nurse here – where is she? (*Shakes him.*) *Where is she?*

BEN: She's a cow. She hit me. (*Covers his head with his hands.*)

JIMMY: I'll knock y'through a wall in a minute, she's my wife, where is she?

BEN: She's . . . she's . . . she's gone out.

(JIMMY *lets go of him.*)

JIMMY: Where's she gone hey? Where? (*Picks* BEN *up again.* BEN *points at the far doorway.*) What about that fuckin' male nurse, Eddie someone, has he gone with her? *ANSWER ME!*

(BEN'*s eyes dart towards* EDDIE, *to* JIMMY, *back to* EDDIE, *then points again in the general direction of the doorway and* EDDIE.)

BEN: He's . . . he's there.

(JIMMY *turns around.* EDDIE *lolling, arms to his knees,* MARIE *sitting in the chair,* PETE *dressed for Hawaii.*)

JIMMY: (*Throws* BEN *away.*) Stupid old sod. (*Goes towards* EDDIE *and* MARIE.) Is there no one here with any sense?

(BEN *giggles then stops suddenly. He giggles again and* EDDIE *joins him.*)

You . . . (*To* MARIE) Have you seen her?

MARIE: She's havin' a baby, an' so am I, look. (*Lifts up her skirt, shows him the cushion.*)

PETE: I'm not, I'm goin' to Hawaii. (*Holds his sign up.*)

JIMMY: Fuckin' Jerusalem!

PETE: Are you a policeman?

JIMMY: Oh aye, sent for the police, have they? That queer-arse Eddie's work that'll be.

PETE: (*Over to* EDDIE) You told them, y' went an' told them, y'lied to me.

JIMMY: Who did? (*Look closely at* EDDIE) An' who're you when you're out?

EDDIE: (*Fast*) Who me, who me? I'm Barry, Barry, Barry.

JIMMY: (*To* PETE) Who is he? You tell me who he is.

PETE: I've got to go now, I'm going to Hawaii, and I'm late.

JIMMY: (*Advancing on him*) Just tell me who he is.

PETE: Er . . .

(JIMMY *grabs hold of* PETE *by his shirt front.*)

Barry! Barry, don't let him get me. (*Drops his bag and sign, tries to protect himself.*) Hit him, Barry!

(JIMMY *lets go of* PETE*'s shirt.*)

JIMMY: (*To himself*) Where the fuck are they?

EDDIE: I know, I know, in there in there, there, there. (*Points at the padded cell.*) Eddie an' Christine, Christine, Christine, nursey, nursey, nursey, ugh ugh ugh shiggy shaggy ugh shaggy shaggy, show you you you. (*Shambles over.*) All the time time time, ugh ugh ugh.

(JIMMY *goes over, shoves the door open, walks inside, no more than enough to close the door.*)

JIMMY: Where? There's no one in here.

(EDDIE *closes the door, locks it fast, puts his head on the door of the cell, closes his eyes.*)

BEN: There is now.

JIMMY: What the . . . hey! You friggin' idiot, let me out, let me out! (*He bangs on the door, fists and feet.*)

EDDIE: I'm sorry.

JIMMY: Y'what? Y'sorr . . . You! You're Eddie!

EDDIE: (*With no sense of victory*) I'm Eddie.

(BEN *is walking over, cackling away.*)

JIMMY: Wait till I get out of here, pal. Y've got no right t'do this to me, I'm not cracked . . . I don't belong here . . . (*Bangs again on the door.*) Let me out, *LET ME OUT!*

BEN: All for the love of a woman. (*Laughs.*) A woman! Y'must be mad, y'deserve t'be in there. She's a cow, she hit me.

PETE: (*As* JIMMY *continues banging*) Right well . . . (*Picks up his bag and his poster.*) Yes well . . . right. (*Coughs.*)

(EDDIE *looks up.*)

EDDIE: (*Flatly*) Are y'going now?

PETE: Yes I am.

EDDIE: Well, good luck, lad, send us a postcard when you get home. (*He puts his arm limply around* PETE.)

(PETE *walks to the door, away from* EDDIE. *Gets there. Stands just outside the room, waits for* EDDIE. *Peeps in, goes out again, coughs wildly.*)

Hey, Peter, come back.

(PETE *hurries back.*)

How far would you be now if I hadn't called you back?

PETE: Just like you, that is, Barry. (*Stands there.*) I'll just y'know go an' have a slash, ready for the road, in case . . . y'know . . .

(EDDIE *does not look up.* PETE *shuffles on his feet and then finally goes off past the nurses' room.*)

JIMMY: (*More soberly*) The police won't do anythin' y'know, she called them out once before; domestic, that's what they call it – take me back to the corner of our road an' drop me – an' as soon as they've gone, I'm comin' back f'you, make sure y' know that, Florence Nightingale.

MARIE: Florence . . .

(*As* EDDIE *talks, she picks the paper up, looks through it for names in the columns.*)

EDDIE: If your wife is leavin' y', it's not for me, you may as well know that much.

JIMMY: (*Confident*) She's not leavin' me, an' she's not goin' anywhere – except home with me.

MARIE: Florence . . . (*Finds the page.*)

EDDIE: I had nothin' to do with . . .

JIMMY: Save y'breath, pal – y'goin' to need it, runnin' away from me. (*He laughs harshly, then is silent.*)

MARIE: Jacqueline . . . Sarah . . . Frederick . . . Damien . . . Barclay . . . Ooooh, Barclay.

BEN: Y'can bank on him. (*Shakes with laughter.*) Bank on him – Barclay. (*Goes across to* MARIE, *looks over her shoulder, down the page.*) You don't want them, girl, they're births. That's what you want, there, 'In Memoriam'.

MARIE: I like Barclay. It's different. Barclay . . .

(PETE *comes back without his bag or his sign. Terrified, wet around his privates. Half screams, half grunts, grabs* EDDIE, *points back towards the door.*)

PETE: Arrr, Arrrr . . . (*High pitched.*) . . . nnnnnn . . . mmmmmmm . . . In . . . in toilets . . . (*Points to ceiling.*) Ve . . . Ve . . . (*Puts his hand around his neck, mimes a rope.*) Vera . . . mmnnnnn . . . neck. *Arrrrr*! *Arrrrrr*! Blood . . . blood . . . on on on on on *her legs*! (*Chokes violently.*)

EDDIE: Oh no, please no. (*Runs towards the doorway and out.*)

(*Pause.*)

BEN: Any Veras in there?

(MARIE *looks down the page.*)

PETE: I was goin', I was, I wasnnnnnnn . . . tonight . . . nnnnn . . . Ha . . . Haw . . . nnnnnnnmmmmmmm.

MARIE: (*Points at the paper.*) Vera.

BEN: (*Reads*) Fairclough, Vera, March 25th, 1986, suddenly, 'Always gentle, never unkind, these are the memories you left behind, My heart aches, my eyes weep, for a wonderful wife I could not keep.' Her loving husband Keith.

MARIE: Keith . . .

JIMMY: What's goin' on out there? Hey you, Eddie, Eddie, *EDDIE!* (*He gives the door a kick.*) Fuck y'then, I can wait.

MARIE: Barclay's better.

BEN: All of them're dead. Dead. Or will be. One day.

(CHRISTINE *returns, walks into the nurses' room, sees Eddie's white coat, looks at his coat hook.* PETE *at the doorway. Enters. Closes the door. Grunts.* BEN *has followed her passage. Moves towards the padded cell.*)

CHRISTINE: Has Eddie gone?

PETE: Nnnnnn . . . (*Nods his head, points out towards the doors, then touches* CHRISTINE *nervously.*)

CHRISTINE: Thought as much. Anyone with him when he went – you know – a man?

(PETE *shakes his head, she looks down at her watch as* PETE *points at the padded cell.*)

Night staff're in now, Peter, they're just coming down. (*Puts her coat on*)

PETE: Vvvvvv . . . (*Swallows.*) Vera.

CHRISTINE: He was with Vera, was he? She give him trouble? (*Looks more closely at him.*) Are you all right?

(*He nods his head.*)

CHRISTINE: Didn't go to Hawaii after all?

(*He shakes his head.*)

Never mind, always tomorrow. (*She picks up her suitcase.*)

PETE: Where . . . where you goin'?

CHRISTINE: Not very far. Not Hawaii, leastways. (*She takes her case, opens the door, goes to walk across the lounge.* MARIE *lost in her list of names.* BEN *giggles as she passes him. He looks at the padded cell, looks at her, she half stops, questions him with a look.*)

BEN: Twat.

(CHRISTINE *smiles, continues walking, goes out.* BEN

watches her go, then turns around towards the cell.)
Y'can come out now, she's gone. (*He giggles, laughs, stops dead.*)
(*Lights out.*)